ESCAPING THE EARL

The League of Rogues - Book 16

LAUREN SMITH

Lauren
SMITH
TIMELESS ROMANCE

ISBN: 978-1-952063-98-5 (e-book edition)

ISBN: 978-1-952063-99-2 (trade paperback edition)

E

xcerpt from the *Quizzing Glass Gazette*, September 21, 1821, the Lady Society column:

IT HAS COME TO THE ATTENTION OF LADY SOCIETY THAT A new titled peer has arrived in London. Ladies, hearken to my words. He is thirty years of age, unmarried, without any mistresses—at least from what this clever listener can glean—and fabulously wealthy. He is also quite handsome, with eyes the color of pale amber and hair as black as a peregrine falcon's wings. Which is fitting, given his name . . .

What is perhaps most surprising is that this gentleman is simply that: a gentleman. It has been a while since I have been witness to a man with charm and grace and selflessness, yet without a wicked bone in his body. Perhaps it is because he never expected to become an earl? If you are husband hunting, seek out this man before some other clever young lady does.

"SOMETHING SIMPLY *MUST* BE DONE ABOUT THAT GIRL."

The hushed, hateful whispers echoed up the stairs to where Sabrina Talleyrand was sitting. She tucked her knees up to her chin as she strained to hear the response from the other person below.

"Yes, yes, Prudence, I know. But we couldn't afford to send her to London for the season when she first came of age, and now she's twenty-two. It's too late for her to be considered for any decent match." Her brother, Jereym, let out a long-suffering sigh.

Prudence, Jereym's wife and Sabrina's sister-in-law, huffed. "She's costly. We are barely making ends meet as it is. We can no longer afford to keep her. You must find a way to marry her off, preferably to someone with deep pockets who will pay off our debts."

"Well, I have good news on that front," Jereym said. "I met a man today at my club. He said he would be interested in meeting her this afternoon, but he's rather a selective man. She may not be up to scratch."

"Nonsense. She's pretty enough—at least to get a man leg-shackled and breed a brat through her."

Prudence's cold tone cut Sabrina deeply. How could

they speak so carelessly, so callously, of her future? She sniffled as tears began to trail down her cheeks.

"When will this gentleman be here, Jereym?"

"Sometime this afternoon. Have a tea service ready, and tell my sister to make herself presentable."

Sabrina stood as she heard the hushed whispers grow louder as Jereym and Prudence moved toward the stairs. It took a moment to wrestle her emotions down and swallow the lump in her throat. She had to buy herself some time to figure out what to do. She wiped her eyes and rushed back to her room. She attempted to busy herself at her small writing desk as Prudence knocked on her door. The last thing she needed was Prudence discovering that she'd become adept at eavesdropping.

"Sabrina, my dear?" Her tone was sickly sweet.

"Yes, Prudence? Do come in."

Her sister-in-law was a tall woman with a willowy figure and china-blue eyes. She would have been pretty if she smiled more and frowned less, but ever since Jereym had married her, Sabrina had rarely seen Prudence in a good mood.

"Oh, Sabrina, good morning." The little mobcap Prudence wore seemed to make her look far older than her twenty-five years. Sabrina vowed she would never wear a cap like that, even if she grew to be ninety.

"Good morning." Sabrina waited, praying her eyes weren't still red.

"Your brother has met someone in London who is

most anxious to meet you. I'm told he's quite handsome, and quite wealthy too. He is coming to visit us today." Prudence plucked a bit of invisible dust from the puffed sleeve of her pink-and-white striped gown. "I believe you should wear your best gown, the orange one."

That wasn't Sabrina's best gown, but Prudence's poor fashion sense was a good thing in this instance, because Sabrina had no desire to look good for this man. If Jereym had found him at his club, that did not speak highly of him. Sabrina loved her brother, but she did not like him very much.

After their parents had died, Jereym had become her guardian, but Jereym could barely look out for himself, let alone her. Had it been possible, Sabrina would have left this house and gone out into the world to take care of herself, but there were so few useful skills she possessed. Her poor sewing skills left dreams of millinery shops and seamstress positions out of the question. And she could not entertain thoughts of those professions she *could* perform, especially those of a more degrading nature.

"Thank you, Prudence. I will change and come downstairs to wait."

"Good, good." Prudence left her, a smug smile twisted on her mouth as she exited the small bedchamber.

Sabrina went to her armoire and stroked her hands along the peeling painted wood. It was one of the last pieces of furniture her brother hadn't sold to pay off his debts. Their drawing room looked passable, as was

Jereym's bedchamber, of course, but the rest of their little cottage was in poor shape. Most of the decent silver and furniture had been sold years ago.

The panels on the armoire were decorated with wildflowers, ones her mother had painted when Sabrina was a child. She traced her fingertips over the snowdrops, dog roses, cornflowers, and bluebells. Their mother had fallen ill a year after their father had died on a hunting trip. Jereym had been a young man then, barely twenty, and she but a girl, and it had changed everything. He had married Prudence and had hoped his new wife's small bit of wealth would sustain them, but Jereym's love of fine clothes and gambling tables had left the three of them worse off than they'd hoped to be. Rather than take out her frustrations with their situation on Jereym, Prudence targeted Sabrina instead.

Sabrina removed the orange gown from the armoire and winced at its blinding color. It was one of Prudence's castoffs. The style was a bit out of date, and the hem needed to be mended. Sabrina had mended it four times already, but her poor sewing skills always left the gown in need of further repairs.

"Miss?" Their single housemaid, Louisa, came into the room. "The master said you might need some help?"

"Oh, yes, thank you." Sabrina was glad to have help as she changed out of her pale-blue muslin gown and into the orange silk day gown. She combed her hair with Louisa's help until it was pulled up and pinned in place. Her dark hair and brown eyes did look all right with the gown after all, but that actually made Sabrina frown. She didn't want to look appealing to whomever Jereym was bringing to meet her.

"Thank you, Louisa." She dismissed the maid, who still had plenty of work to see to. It was one more thing that Sabrina wasn't pleased about. They had been forced to dismiss all but a handful of their servants. It wasn't because she liked to be waited upon hand and foot, but rather because most of the staff were friends, and seeing them leave to find work elsewhere had hurt. And those left behind had found their duties doubled. Louisa had stayed on, acting as an upstairs maid and housekeeper, and one footman had stayed, shouldering the responsibilities of the butler as well. They also still retained their cook and one gardener.

By the time Sabrina summoned the courage to go downstairs, she was sick to her stomach. The next few hours became a painful lesson in patience and perseverance as she sat in the drawing room trying to read.

It was all such nonsense. Sitting and waiting for a man to change her life, likely not for the better. She had a thousand other things she could be doing at that moment. She'd never been one to be idle, except when she was reading, which of late she had done a fair amount of. Before they'd lost most of their money, she'd baked bread and prepared other food in baskets for the local elderly neighbors and the poorer farmers nearby.

She'd even assisted the local schoolmaster in teaching some of the female children whose parents couldn't afford to send them to school. Mr. Wilson had been kind enough to allow her the use of a separate room to teach the girls, and she did it without expectation of any payment. She believed in education for both boys and girls, and if she could offer her help, she would teach without charge.

"Master, you have a visitor," the footman announced.

Jereym stood up, excitement clear in his eyes as he told the footman to show their visitor in. A tall man entered the drawing room a moment later. He was fair-haired, slender, and rather delicate for a man, but in a way that would make him rather attractive to some ladies.

Her brother puffed up with pride as he shook the man's hand. "Simon, welcome. Please let me introduce you to my wife, Prudence, and my sister, Sabrina. Prudence, Sabrina, this is Simon Booker."

"Welcome, Mr. Booker," Prudence purred. "Do come in. We were just about to have some tea." She reached for the silver bell beside her chair and rang it a little overzealously. Under other circumstances, Sabrina would have laughed, but not right then.

"Thank you for the warm welcome." He sat down beside Sabrina on the settee, and she tried to scoot away from him. Her brother shot her a glare.

"Miss Talleyrand, your brother spoke highly of you, but he failed to tell me of your beauty." Mr. Booker spoke with an eagerness that made her uneasy. The look in his eyes was unsettling, as though he were examining a horse he was anxious to buy. It was a possessive look that made her stomach turn.

"Oh, thank you." Sabrina, wildly uncomfortable, still did not wish to be rude to this man. She was not the sort of woman to be ungracious, even when facing something detestable.

"I know it heartens a lady greatly to hear her looks spoken so highly of," Mr. Booker said with a proud smile.

Sabrina fisted her skirts, nearly shredding the thread-bare satin. He was admitting to giving her compliments just to put her in a good mood?

"So, Simon, how long will you be in this part of the country?" her brother asked.

"A few days, and then I must return to London." But his gaze slid meaningfully to Sabrina, and she could picture her brother and this man at his club in London planning this very interaction.

"Oh, heavens, I just realized, I must tell our cook something very important about this evening's meal." Sabrina jumped to her feet, causing her brother and Mr. Booker to rise as well.

"I'm sure whatever it is, it's *not* important at all," Jereym said firmly.

"Oh, but it is. I shall return shortly. Please excuse me." She ducked into the corridor and caught her breath at a sudden rush of panic at leaving. She'd thought for a moment her brother might try to stop her, but he hadn't.

Sabrina rushed out of the house then and into the gardens behind the cottage as fast as she could without breaking into a run. There was no way she was going to sit there and *endure* more of that. Yes, that was the right word for the torture that visit would have been. She'd only made it halfway through the garden before she heard someone running after her. She turned and saw it was Mr. Booker.

"Drat," she muttered as she slowed enough to let him catch up with her.

"Miss Talleyrand, I hope you don't mind me joining you. It will give us a chance to get better acquainted if we are to . . ." He suddenly stopped speaking.

She stopped walking altogether. "If we are to what, sir?" she asked quietly.

"Well, you must be aware of my reason for being here. I am in need of a wife, and your brother assured me you would be most willing, given your financial situation."

Sabrina closed her eyes and pinched the bridge of her nose. "Mr. Booker, we may indeed be facing difficulties, but I'm not prepared to marry you—or frankly anyone. Please understand I mean it as no insult. I simply don't wish to marry."

She actually would have loved to be married, but to a man who adored her for who she was and whom she felt the same way toward.

"Oh, I do understand. But I require an heir to continue my line, and you will do quite well giving me one."

An heir? Was he serious? Surely not.

She tried to keep her temper reined in. "Sir, I'm not a broodmare." She was not a woman prone to shouting or getting openly upset, but this man seemed to know just what to say to provoke her.

His face reddened. "I disagree. The most important thing a lady can offer is her breeding abilities."

"I'm not a creature to breed, sir. That is the end of it." She said this with such finality she hoped she truly had put an end to the matter.

Instead, the last of Mr. Booker's civility vanished. "You will be my wife. You will bear me an heir; or else I will call in your brother's debts. He owes me quite a lot of money, you see."

For a moment, she simply stared at him, stunned. He was going to blackmail her?

"I do see, and he is the one indebted to you, not me."

Mr. Booker grasped her arm tightly when she tried to walk away. "*You* are the form of payment I expect," he warned. "I tried to be polite, but you are proving that you don't deserve my best behavior." He jerked her toward him and slammed his mouth over hers.

Sabrina froze for a heartbeat, then shoved him back and swung a balled fist. She hit him square in the jaw hard enough that he let go of her.

"Why, you little—"

Sabrina ran before she could hear what else he said.

She sprinted into the woods behind the cottage. He didn't come after her, but she didn't dare stop running.

When she finally stopped, her lungs were burning, her eyes were blurry with tears, and her hair was streaming down in wild waves. She sagged against a tree and sank to the ground, shaking. Had she truly just been accosted by that man?

Sabrina waited at least an hour before making the walk back home, and she deeply regretted it when she did. Her brother was waiting for her.

"Where the devil have you been?" he snapped. "Mr. Booker waited for you for more than an hour, and when you didn't return, he left here furious."

"As he should. That man—for he is no *gentleman*—accosted me, Jereym. *Against* my wishes."

Her brother looked momentarily uncertain before his gaze hardened. He'd once been such a handsome man, but living on the edge had made him age in the last few years.

"You have no idea of the position you have put me in. My wishes are what matter here, and they are to be obeyed. I owe that man quite a large sum of money. Now that he has seen you, he has made up his mind that he wants you. If I give you to him, I'll settle my debts completely."

Sabrina's mouth ran dry as she stared at her brother in horror. "No, no, Jereym! You cannot force me to marry him."

"I absolutely can. You have no choice. A doctor will be

here tomorrow morning to inspect the state of your maidenhead, as per Mr. Booker's request."

"My maidenhead . . ." Words failed Sabrina. The man wanted her to be a virgin?

"Yes. He insisted he will only marry a virgin. I have assured him that you are untouched, but he insisted that a doctor confirm it. So tomorrow morning you will present yourself for inspection."

"Father would never have done this to me," Sabrina said quietly. "Never." She was torn between rage and despair that her own brother would *sell* her like this.

"Father is dead." The words were delivered more harshly than any slap Jereym might have ever given her.

"How could you?" Sabrina hated the fresh tears that stung her eyes. After five years, she thought she'd become accustomed to this. But she hadn't, not really.

A shadow of doubt passed over Jereym's face, but it quickly vanished. "Go to your room. I don't wish to see you at dinner."

Sabrina rushed up the stairs and into her room, slamming the door so hard that it rattled in the frame. Then she threw herself upon her bed and buried her face in the blankets. A long time later, when she lay exhausted, she could hear voices downstairs. The house's thin walls were her allies, it seemed. They always warned her of danger. Jereym and Prudence were somewhere one floor below, speaking.

"I thought we were to attend the ball at Lady Germain's tonight," Prudence whined.

"Not tonight. I am in a foul mood," Jereym growled.

"But my dear, it is a masquerade. You know how I enjoy those . . ."

The conversation died out as Jereym and Prudence moved out of her hearing. But it didn't matter. Sabrina had found a way out. She'd thought at first to simply run away, but now she had a way to make sure that tomorrow morning she would not have her *precious* maidenhead and Mr. Booker would leave her alone for good.

She slid out of bed and once more opened her armoire. She had one gown worthy of a masquerade, her mother's court gown. It was silver silk and pearls with a silver-threaded embroidered bodice. She pulled on the bell cord to summon Louisa. When the maid arrived, she clasped the girl's hands in her own.

"Louisa, I need your help. I must leave tonight for a few hours. If my brother or Prudence asks after me, can you tell them that I am ill?"

"Yes," Louisa said.

She embraced the maid. "Thank you."

"Now, let me help you change, miss." Louisa assisted Sabrina as she changed into the silver satin gown. Sabrina was lucky enough to have a masquerade mask that had also belonged to her mother. It was a gold-and-silver glittering thing that had exquisite decorations painted on it.

It also covered most of her face except for her mouth and chin. A perfect disguise.

Once she was ready to leave, Louisa kept watch in the corridor so that Sabrina could escape to the front door of the cottage and leave. It would be a long walk to the Germain estate, but if she left early enough she should reach the grand manor house just in time for the ball to start.

2

Peregrine Ashby was incredibly grateful for the protection of his domino as he watched the crowds flow across the ballroom in Lady Germain's grand manor house. The mask allowed him to move through the well-dressed people with more anonymity than he'd had in the last few weeks.

As the new Earl of Rutland, he'd risen from a somewhat obscure gentleman to a man with far too much popularity, in his opinion. Most of it had to do with the Lady Society column posted in the *Quizzing Glass Gazette*. She'd told the unmarried ladies of London far too much about him, despite her attempt not to name him directly.

After his great-uncle Frederick had died, the earldom had passed to him. It was entirely unexpected. There had been at least three other gentlemen ahead of him, yet all of those men had also died in the last year. All three of them had been together on a small cutter ship that had sunk off the coast of Egypt, and all lives were lost.

Now at thirty years of age, Peregrine had opportunities in abundance. He had moved out of his cramped bachelor residence in a rough part of London and into his great-uncle's townhouse in Grosvenor Square. He'd also inherited the family estate, Ashbridge Heath, in the Cotswolds, and though he had not visited it yet, he'd been corresponding with the butler and housekeeper there. He hoped to see it in a few weeks' time, but until then, he was enjoying himself here as much as he could.

"Ashby? That you?" a familiar voice greeted him. He saw a tall blond-haired man wearing a dark-blue domino striding toward him through the crowd. Despite the mask, Peregrine recognized his friend. Those bright-blue eyes were unmistakable, along with that wicked smirk that promised trouble.

"Lennox, keep your voice down," Peregrine said as Rafe Lennox joined him at the back of the crowded ballroom.

"What? Afraid someone will recognize you?" Rafe asked.

"Yes, exactly," Peregrine grumbled. For the last three weeks, it seemed he had dodged every young female and scheming mother in London and the surrounding boroughs. That was not an easy thing to do, but he was determined to avoid marriage, at least for the time being. He was in no hurry to get leg-shackled. He'd only just been given a new life, and if he was burdened with a wife, he feared he would be obliged to stay at home, or at the least feel duty-bound to stay home. He was also wary of English society for the moment. He'd been at the bottom of society for many years and had been treated poorly. Now he was out of his depth in his new position, and he needed to take the time to sort out the good from the bad in the upper echelons of the *ton*.

When he did eventually have to marry, he wanted to marry someone he could tolerate. Until then, he just wanted his freedom, and marriage was the opposite of that. At least, it had been for his parents. Neither of them had liked each other, and they'd lived much of their lives as far apart as possible, even while under the same roof. And given how little money his father had had to support them, this had been most of the time.

It became easier when his mother died, because his father's temperament had softened a little. But he had died not long thereafter, leaving Peregrine entirely alone.

Rafe jovially put an arm around Peregrine's shoulder and hollered at the people nearby. "We've got Lord Rutland here." He pointed at a gaggle of girls. "You lot, line up and be ready to dance with him."

Peregrine rammed an elbow none too gently into Rafe's stomach.

Rafe doubled over, his breath escaping in a rush. "Bloody hell, man. I was only teasing."

"Yes, well, now you've outed me, and those ladies look

ready to hunt me down and mount my head on their mantels."

The young women Rafe had so recklessly shouted at were now huddled together, their fans flapping and their heads bent as they whispered to each other. Occasionally one girl would glance at Peregrine over her shoulder.

"Christ, they do look rather serious, don't they?" Rafe smoothed his waistcoat out as he now eyed the ladies in return with no small amount of trepidation.

"I think, given how you're raising that adorable little ward of yours, that *you* should be the one to get married, Lennox."

"What? The devil take you, man. Marriage is not for me. The world is full of women in need of a proper kiss, and it is my solemn duty to provide myself to them. Besides," Rafe chuckled, "Isla would never be content to share her new papa with any woman."

It never ceased to amaze Peregrine that Rafe, a man known for his devil-may-care attitude, had returned from visiting Scotland with a small child in tow. More surprising was the fact that she was not his by blood, but he'd taken her in as his daughter all the same. Fatherhood had wrought many positive changes in the notorious rogue, but he would always be a brave and irresponsible trouble-maker as well as a damned loyal friend.

"Well, given that you caused this mess, I believe you ought to do the honorable thing and throw yourself upon the sword for me." Peregrine pushed Rafe into the crowd of young ladies who had broken up their little war council and were headed toward him.

Rafe wobbled comically as he stumbled through the pack of husband hunters, giving Peregrine a moment to duck out of sight. He used the tall marble pillars in the ballroom to hide and moved far enough away that the pack could not find him so easily. He reached the orchestra at the back of the ballroom near the doors, where a servant was announcing the newly arriving guests.

This glittering world of silks and gold-tinged laughter was still so new to him. He hadn't grown up with the luxuries one expected an earl to have. His great-uncle had held out hope for another heir, any one of his sons or their children, but none had survived. It was only him, the son of a lesser son in their noble line. Peregrine had never even met his great-uncle Frederick. Yet he was prepared to do his duty and fit into this world. He knew all the dances, the modes for proper address, and table manners, but that didn't make him feel suitable as a peer of the realm. That was all the young women here tonight saw: his lands, his title, and his fortune. Not him.

I wish for one night to be seen as just a man—as myself.

A few more guests entered the ballroom, each of them announced, all except the last one, a young woman. She waved the servant away with a polite smile when he inquired her name. It was a bold move, one that caught Peregrine's attention. Fascinated, he studied the woman. Her gown was a silver silk creation that seemed to glow beneath the lamplight. Hundreds of pearls covered her bodice, capped sleeves, and the silver outer skirts of her gown. Her hair was piled atop her head in delicate curls, with silver ribbon running through the strands.

She tilted her head to one side and he saw that her mask was a soft gold and silver. He could only guess at her features above her lips, but the rest of her was regal and yet almost dreamlike. She seemed like a fae queen destined to marry a handsome fae prince. She was incomparable to the mere mortals around her, so much so that as she walked deeper into the room, the crowd parted around her. Ladies bowed their heads, and men did the same.

Who *was* she?

Peregrine moved into the shadows, keeping pace with her slow progress into the room. Just as the music ended, he moved toward her. He was barely aware of his feet until the moment he reached her. Where other men dared not tread, he now boldly stepped forward. He had come here to dance, after all, and one dance did not mean he would have to marry this mysterious beauty, whoever she was.

"A dance, my lady?" he asked, then bowed before straightening and holding out a hand to her. She hesitated, her dark-brown eyes fathomless, her lips parted as she drew in a quick breath before she responded.

"Thank you." She placed her palm in his, and a spark of something shot between them.

He led her onto the dance floor, never more thankful

that Lady Germain had forgone dance cards to allow for people to dance with whomever they wished, and to maintain some mystery with their masks.

He swept the woman into his arms as the musicians began a waltz. He didn't worry about the steps as he guided her across the floor.

"You dance beautifully," she said as they moved as one.

"As do you, my lady." He sought her eyes, and she looked away as though shy. Such a contrast to the bold woman who had arrived through the door unannounced.

Who could she be? A clever debutante, a widowed woman, a spinster seeking a night of excitement? Whoever she was, she had set fire to the imaginations of everyone in the ballroom tonight, himself included. He'd never been a romantic man, but something about this woman left him with dreams of gardens and dances at midnight through the roses and wisteria.

"Will you tell me your name?" he asked.

"I thought it was supposed to be a mystery," she remarked with a melancholy smile.

He recognized in her a kindred spirit. Whoever she was, she wished to be left alone by the world, and tonight would be her only escape. A sudden fear that she would vanish in his arms like mist the moment the dance ended set him on edge.

"You'll stay for another dance?" he asked as they twirled past a crowd of young women who looked on in envy. "Or will you vanish, my fae queen?"

"I may do either," she laughed. "What can you offer me to stay, dear mortal? Tempt me," she commanded in a soft, enchanting voice.

"Let me see . . . I could entertain you with jokes. Or perhaps riddles? A walk in the gardens?" He would have offered her everything he had to give, even his heart. But this was merely madness born of infatuation, that was all. Love at first sight was nonsense. It was a story told to debutantes before they faced their first balls. It did not exist for a thirty-year-old gentleman.

"A walk in the gardens . . . and perhaps a riddle or two?"

"Done, my lady."

Peregrine escorted her off the dance floor as the waltz ended. It seemed as though everyone was still watching them.

"Heavens, we are being watched most diligently, aren't we?" she mused.

"Yes, it's rather irritating. Give me a moment." He studied the various exits. "Come, let us fetch some ratafia and make our escape out the doors just beyond the refreshment tables."

They retrieved the drinks and began to move slowly backward toward the open terrace doors.

"Almost there," Peregrine murmured as they stood on the threshold. "No sudden moves now . . ." The fall breeze came through the white curtains which had been pulled back to the edges of the doors.

The woman took another sip of her drink. "On three?"

He nodded. "One . . . two . . . *three.*" And they plunged swiftly out onto the terrace together.

He pulled her down the steps that led to the gardens. "Come, this way." They set their glasses on the terrace railing as they left. She laughed as she picked up her skirts with her free hand and followed him. They sprinted across the perfectly manicured lawn and vanished into the tall hedges. Only when the house was no longer visible did they stop.

"I believe we are quite safe to enjoy our walk in peace." Peregrine tucked her arm in his. "Now, I believe I promised you a riddle, did I not?"

"You did."

Rather enjoying himself, he tapped his chin. "What walks on four feet in the morning, two in the afternoon, and three at night?"

She grinned. "I asked for a riddle, not a history lesson. If I remember correctly, that is the riddle of the Sphinx from *Oedipus Rex* . . . and the answer is *man.* As an infant, he crawls on all fours, as an adult he walks on two legs, and when he is old, he uses a walking stick."

"Ah, I forgot I was matching wits with an ancient fae. Very well . . . What of this one?" Then he recited a poem:

As I was going to St. Ives,
Upon the road I met seven wives,
Each wife had seven sacks,
Each sack had seven cats,

Each cat had seven kits:
Kits, cats, sacks and, wives,
How many were there going to St. Ives?

"Oh dear, would you tell it to me again?" she asked.

Peregrine dutifully repeated the riddle.

"May I ask a question?"

"Of course."

"I assume this person going to St. Ives is traveling upon a road and is not going faster or slower than any other travelers upon the road and is alone when he first sets out?"

It took Peregrine a moment to think the questions through as they related to the answer.

"Yes. Your assumptions are correct."

She hesitated only a moment before answering. "One. One is going to St. Ives. The others mentioned are a mathematical misdirection. One would assume he could only pass these other travelers as they passed by him coming from the opposite direction."

"Well done, my fae queen. Very well done. Would you like one more?"

"Yes, and be careful—if you choose one that's too easy, I shall vanish forever." She laughed.

"Very well. It is a short one but a very hard one. There are two doors, one leading to heaven and one leading to hell. Each one has an identical guard. You may ask one guard one question and then make your choice as to which door to pass through, with your goal to enter the gate to heaven. One of the guards always tells the truth and one always lies. What question would you ask of which guard?"

They stopped by a white marble bench and sat down beside each other. Peregrine was lost in the beauty of the moonlight upon her alabaster skin.

"Now that is difficult," she said. "I would ask either guard what the other guard would say, then go through the opposite door."

"My God," Peregrine murmured. "You've heard of that one too?"

"No, but it is logical. Sometimes the answer to a riddle is the easiest solution one can manage. Assuming one does not overthink it."

She stood and walked farther down the path, and he followed.

"My lady, please tell me your name." He reached for her hand, pulling it into his own and stroking his fingertips over the inside of her palm. She took in a breath as he pressed a kiss against her inner wrist. She started to tremble, and he nearly forgot himself and tried to wrap his arms around her. He stopped at the last minute and instead released her hand, and she seemed to calm.

She chuckled softly as she composed herself. "I'm sorry. I cannot tell you. Even if I did, it would do neither of us any good."

"Why?"

She looked up at the endless inky black sky. "Because

after tomorrow, I shall be no one." She stood and started to walk away

Peregrine went after her and caught her hand, halting her. "You frighten me with your talk of becoming no one on the morrow. Why do you say this?"

She turned her face away, but when he gently turned her back to look at him, tears trailed down the edge of her mask.

"You're crying," he breathed. His concern for this woman he didn't know twisted him inside until he felt an almost physical pain. He'd never felt so connected to anyone in his life, and yet she was an utter stranger. But in that moment, it was the truth. He *was* connected to her somehow.

"I am, but it does not matter."

"It doesn't? Then what does, my lady?"

She cupped his face and rose up on her tiptoes. "This . . ."

She kissed him, and the world around that kiss ceased to be.

3

S abrina could think of only one way to distract this man before her. She grabbed him and kissed him. She'd never kissed a man before and therefore had no idea how it should feel, but her initial clumsiness faded as the mysterious man pulled her closer and his lips eagerly met hers. He was so tall, so wonderfully warm and hard against her own body as she leaned into him. The man kept her within the circle of his embrace, leaving her feeling safe in a way she hadn't imagined possible. She surrendered herself to him, hoping the kiss would last forever.

She quickly learned how to move her mouth, how to savor the sensations and the tingle of excitement the kiss sent through her entire body. When he licked at the seam of her lips, she pulled back a little, startled.

"Easy, my darling, I don't wish to frighten you. Open your mouth for me."

"Open my mouth?" She reluctantly moved back into his arms, uncertain if she would like this or not.

"Trust me." He brushed the backs of his fingers down the side of her throat in a tender caress. She did trust him. It was strange . . . but it was also true. She trusted this man.

Their mouths met once again and she opened to him, gasping as his tongue touched hers, light and playful. It was exciting, forbidden, and far above what she'd imagined kissing would be. She decided right then that she enjoyed it. The man held her close, kissing her as the stars moved slowly overhead.

But she needed more. She needed this man to claim her tonight so that tomorrow she would be free of her brother and Mr. Booker.

When they broke apart for air, he nuzzled the crown of her hair. Her whole body quivered with nerves as she asked him the question that would change her life forever.

"Would you make love to me beneath the stars?"

For a moment, only the crickets could be heard.

"Beg pardon?"

"Please, I do not have time to explain, but I would like it very much if you could."

She watched confusion war with desire on his face.

"Are you trying to trick me into compromising you? Is your father or mother hiding in the hedges to discover us?" His tone was less warm than before. There was cold suspicion in his beautiful tawny-colored eyes.

"No!" Sabrina answered.

"Then why . . . ?"

Could she tell him? Would he understand? In the end, she felt she had no choice but to trust him. "A man I detest is blackmailing my family, and the only way he can be satisfied is by marrying me. But he will only take me if I am untouched. He even has a doctor who is coming in the morning to examine the state of my virtue. I should like it very much to be *touched* by you. Please . . ."

"Christ, how did you end up with a man like that who would—?"

"It was not by choice, I assure you. I am a victim of ill fate, and I fear this may be my only chance of escape."

"You truly want this?" he asked, still hesitant. His arms were still around her, still letting her feel safe against his tall, muscled body. He had every reason to suspect she was trying to catch him in a parson's mousetrap, yet she could tell he believed her.

"Yes. Even though we are strangers, I trust you."

He chuckled dryly. "This is not how I envisioned my evening proceeding, but I am honored to be chosen to save you in such a fashion."

"Where should we . . . ?" She didn't know where best to accomplish the deed.

"Come." He led her past the gardens and into a meadow. No one would venture this far from the house.

They would not be disturbed. He removed his coat and laid it upon the ground for her.

"May I?" He offered her his hand as she eased to the ground and lay back upon his coat. The fabric was still warm, and his scent clung to it. The aroma was dark, with hints of sandalwood and leather. He must ride often. The thought of him astride some powerful beast, his thighs tightening as he guided it, made her body tight and flush with heat.

He lay down beside her and leaned over to kiss her again. She was lost to him and the pleasure of his mouth over hers. She wasn't aware at first that he was sliding a hand up her skirts until she felt the breeze against her bare thighs. She tensed and he paused, one hand resting on her outer thigh.

"Are you all right?" He was so masculine, so in command of his body and hers in that moment. They hadn't even begun to make love, yet he had the consideration to ask how she felt. His care for her challenged everything she'd come to expect from this moment.

She nodded. "Yes, please continue. I'm a little nervous, that's all."

His mouth moved to her neck, and he played with the ribbons on her stockings as he slid his hand up into her undergarments. She opened her legs a little more, and when his fingertips brushed her sex, she gasped and threw her head back.

"That's it, my darling. Relax and let me touch you. Enjoy how it feels."

Sensations spiraled through her, and she whimpered in anticipation each time he touched her.

"I don't wish to hurt you," he murmured. "But it may hurt this first time."

"Yes, I know." She relaxed as he continued to touch her. When he pressed a fingertip inside her, it was tight but she welcomed his gentleness. He continued to rub his finger inside her until the wetness there increased and she relaxed a little. She circled her hips, and his finger sank deeper.

Then he withdrew his hand and unfastened his trousers. "I wish we had more time. I want to kiss every inch of you."

"I want that too, but we haven't time." She cupped his cheek, and he leaned down to steal one more kiss as he settled between her spread thighs and pressed inside her. The sudden pinch of pain faded as he continued to kiss her. Then he filled her—that was the only word to describe it. The sensation of no ending and no beginning between them.

He rocked his body against hers, and she wrapped her arms around his neck, holding on to him as something wondrous built between them.

"Can you see the stars?" he asked as they moved together.

Her eyes lifted to gaze at the blanket of stars above them, and it was the most beautiful sight she'd ever seen.

"I wish you could see them," she said.

"I do, my darling. I see them reflected in your eyes."

She threaded her fingers in his hair and touched the black ribbons that held his mask to his face. She wished she could pull it off and see his features. Was his face as handsome as the rest of him? His jaw was strong and straight; there was no weak aristocratic double chin or placid jawline. Gentle mischief gleamed in his whiskey-colored eyes. He seemed handsome, but she could not be certain, not without seeing him without his mask.

But he would have to remain a mystery. They both needed the anonymity. If she were to ever see him again, even if she were free, as she hoped to be, it would only hurt her heart. They would have this one moment, this one night. The heat building in her lower belly began to intensify, and she felt some strange wildness come upon her. It frightened her a little.

"My lord . . . I feel faint," she whispered. It felt as if she were falling, as if she might . . . die. Was that possible?

"Do you wish for me to stop?" he asked.

"No, don't stop. Please, *never* stop." If she was about to die, she would enjoy this with her last breath.

He moved more urgently, his body thrusting against hers. She gripped his shoulders as that wildness overtook her. She was so stunned by the fierce rush of pleasure that she cried out. He covered her mouth with his, drinking in the sound. Their lips broke apart a moment later as he gave a shout of his own. Something hot flooded her womb, and she curled her legs tight about his waist, afraid he would suddenly sever the connection between them before she was ready to let him go.

They stayed fused together for some time before he moved away. He removed a handkerchief from his coat and gently cleaned her and himself. Her virgin's blood was a dark smear upon the white cloth in the moonlit sky.

"Did I hurt you very much?" he asked.

"Not much. It felt quite magnificent at the end." She was glad the mask hid most of her blush and the night hid the rest.

"Would you like to go back inside now?" he asked.

"Can we stay just a moment longer and watch the stars?" Sabrina wanted desperately for this moment not to end.

"Of course." He sat beside her, and they gazed up at the night sky. He reached over and covered one of her hands with his. She wasn't sure why tonight of all nights she needed this, to be out beneath the night sky watching the stars flicker in their celestial distance. It was as though a season of her life had passed this night, and a great change would soon be upon her.

She was afraid of that coming change. It would be a harsh winter—she could feel it deep in her bones. But tonight, it was like a late-summer eve where winter was but a distant dream yet to come.

"Thank you for tonight, my lord." She finally got to her feet. He retrieved his coat and, after beating the grass off it, put it back on.

"I wish . . . I wish I could do more for you, my lady," he said. The honesty was so clear in his voice that she knew he meant it.

"You've saved me from a terrible fate. It is enough."

"Will you let me walk you back?" he asked.

She nodded and accepted his arm. Whatever came tomorrow, she would always have her memory of this night to warm her heart.

PEREGRINE WALKED THE MYSTERIOUS BEAUTY BACK TO the ballroom. He studied her face a long moment, wishing he could see her features clearly, but he could tell that she was beautiful. He could hear it in her voice and see it in the way she carried herself. Even if her face was unremarkable by other men's standards, Peregrine knew this woman was the world's most beautiful. His own personal Helen of Troy, destined to ruin him.

In this one brief encounter, she had made him rethink his stance on marriage and settling down. And that was so very dangerous. That was how his father had felt when he'd met his mother, that marrying her would be everything he'd dreamed, and she had imagined the same. But they had both been gravely mistaken in their beliefs. Love and marriage were no recipe for happiness. They were a condemnation, a prison sentence.

He nodded toward the refreshment table. "Please, let me fetch you a drink. You must be thirsty."

She smiled at him, and his stomach fluttered wildly. "Thank you, I'd like that."

"Stay here. I shall return." He went briskly to the refreshment table and collected two glasses. Then he returned . . . only to find she wasn't there. He glanced around, searching the crowd for the beauty in a stunning silver gown.

She'd vanished, just as he'd feared.

"Who was that enchanting woman you were with?" Rafe asked as he joined him.

"I don't know."

"What do you mean, you don't know? You danced with her. You must have at least introduced yourselves."

Peregrine shook his head. "She never said her name, not even when I asked. My God . . . she's truly gone. I'm beginning to wonder if I dreamed it."

"If I hadn't seen you dance with her, along with half of London's highest society, I would have to agree. But you did dance with her, she does exist, and everyone is simply buzzing with questions about her."

A middle-aged raven-haired beauty approached Peregrine and Rafe.

"Lord Rutland, who was that enchanting creature you danced with?"

"You see?" Rafe said.

"You do not know her, Lady Germain?" Peregrine asked.

She laughed and pulled away her black-and-red mask, which she held on a stick. "No, but I wish I did. I have run my mind over all the young ladies I issued invitations to, and I cannot think of who she is."

"Did you see where she went?"

"I can't say that I did."

"A veritable mystery," Rafe said. "Oh, this is delicious."

Peregrine continued to search the ballroom for the woman in the silver gown, but he did not find her. Perhaps she really was a fae queen and had slipped back into her twilight realm as easily as mist fading before the dawn.

4

The following morning, Sabrina paced nervously in her bedchamber as she waited for the doctor to arrive. Mr. Booker and her brother were below in the drawing room, already planning her future.

They would certainly be shocked when the doctor pronounced her impure.

What a revolting word, meant to shame and belittle an entire sex for actions that men enjoyed without consequence. She felt no more soiled or damaged than yesterday. What she and the mysterious stranger had done last night had felt quite the opposite of impure. It had been something that came out of need, and yet so much more had been found there. Two lonely souls coming together.

"Stop pacing," Prudence barked as they heard a rider approach outside. Sabrina rushed to the window and saw an old man climb off his horse and vanish as he approached the cottage door.

A few minutes later, there was a knock upon her bedchamber door, and Prudence let the man inside.

He squinted at Prudence through thick spectacles. "Which of you shall I be inspecting?"

Prudence jabbed a finger at Sabrina. "Her."

"Ah, yes. Miss, would you kindly lie back upon the bed?"

Sabrina did as he asked. Inside she was seething and mortified that this man would soon be touching her for no other reason than to suit Mr. Booker's desire for a virgin bride.

"Please move closer to the edge of the bed," the doctor said. "Knees up, legs spread. I shall be as gentle as possible."

She winced as his hands probed her, but he was gentler than she'd expected. He thrust a fingertip inside her, and she winced, still sore from last night.

"Miss, have you had relations with a man before?" the doctor asked.

"I have," Sabrina said.

"She's lying," Prudence snapped.

The doctor looked between her and Prudence. "Madam, I can quite easily tell that her maidenhead is not there. If she says she has been with a man, she certainly has."

Hate-filled eyes settled upon Sabrina. "Are you positive?"

"Quite certain." The doctor removed his hand from between her legs. "You may sit up, miss. I am finished."

Prudence seemed at a loss for words, and then she stormed out of the room. The doctor smiled apologetically at Sabrina.

"You seem relieved, my dear."

"I am. I took great pains to avoid marrying one of the gentlemen you met downstairs."

The doctor's face tensed. "I suspected as much. Most young ladies would have lied under such circumstances." He collected his coat. "Good luck, miss. I fear you shall need it."

After the doctor left the room, she rushed to the door and locked it. Within a minute, there was shouting and steps thundered up the stairs.

The door rattled ominously. "Sabrina, open this door at once! You hear me?"

"Yes, you little whore, open up!" Mr. Booker shouted.

Numb with terror as to the consequences of her actions, Sabrina had only one thought. To run. She collected her reticule, the small amount of money she had saved, her mother's silver court gown, as well as a single spare gown, and tucked them into her valise. She rushed to the window. There was a latticework of climbing roses and ivy beneath her, and she began to climb down with her small valise in one hand. When she was close enough to the ground, she let the valise drop, then climbed the rest of the way down.

Thorns from the roses and slivers of the old lattice scratched and pricked her arms and legs, but she didn't stop. It wouldn't be long before her brother and Mr. Booker broke into her room and discovered her missing. She grabbed her valise from the ground and rounded the cottage until she reached the stables. Their only groom, a young man named Kenneth, was feeding the horses. He jumped to attention when he saw her.

"Miss Talleyrand!"

"Kenneth, could you saddle Celeste quickly?" she asked.

"Yes, miss." He rushed to put a saddle on her dappled gray mare. Then he boosted her up and attached her valise to the saddle behind her.

"Kenneth, you never saw me. Do you understand?"

He nodded, understanding what she meant. "I never saw anyone this afternoon. Got no idea how Celeste got out of her stall neither."

She dug in her heels and rode Celeste hard until they were well away from the once cozy cottage that had been her home.

It was nightfall before she stopped riding, and the only place for food and lodging was a rather shabby coaching inn. She found a stable boy, who took Celeste, and then she crossed the cobblestoned courtyard toward the inn.

With each step, she felt her fear and exhaustion threatening to overwhelm her.

What had she been thinking to run away? She had enough money to survive for a few weeks before she would need to find a position to support herself and Celeste.

She rubbed her arms and cursed herself for not thinking to grab a cloak. "I am a fool . . ." It was early fall, and the cold nights could become rather chilly.

She pushed the door open and cringed as she saw the inn was even shabbier inside than it was outside. The tables were unkempt, and the few guests inside looked decidedly dangerous. But she couldn't leave. Celeste needed a stall, fresh hay, water, and a warm blanket after being pushed so hard today. So Sabrina would do what she must to keep her horse healthy and well.

"Can I 'elp you, miss?" the barmaid asked.

"Oh, yes, thank you. Are there any rooms available? I would also like some supper, if that's possible."

"It is. This way." The maid escorted her to the bar, where a rotund woman was seeing to several men by filling their mugs with ale.

"Mrs. Jeffries, this lady needs a room and supper, if'n you don't mind."

Mrs. Jeffries let out a huff, dislodging a gray lock of hair from her mouth.

"Right then. Take her things up to the last room, number seven."

"Yes, Mrs. Jeffries." The maid jerked her head toward the stairs. "This way, miss."

Sabrina was escorted to a small room with a tiny bed and no fireplace. It was drab, and yet it wasn't unlike the one she had just left at her home.

"That'll be three shillings, miss." The maid held out a hand, and Sabrina parted with her money.

"I'll be up shortly with some stew." The maid left her to get settled, not that there was much settling to do. She set her valise on the floor and sat down on the bed with a heavy sigh. Across the hall, she heard a child's sudden giggle. Curious, she went to the door and cracked it open. A tall blond-haired man, far too attractive to be safe for any woman, held the hand of an adorable little girl. She wore a light-blue gown that was in the height of fashion, even for a child so young.

"Here we are, my darling. This one is us." They stopped at the door across from her.

"Hello!" The little girl greeted Sabrina and waved a tiny hand at her. She couldn't have been more than six.

"Hello." Sabrina greeted the girl warmly, then blushed when she met the eyes of the man. "You have a beautiful daughter," she said.

The man chuckled. "Thank you. The little mite is adorable, isn't she?" Sabrina wasn't used to such a handsome man looking at her like that, but she didn't sense that he meant her harm. Certainly not with such a precious thing in tow. He reminded her of the mystery man at the ball, but that man had golden-amber eyes and dark hair. Still, this man did make her feel that same sense of safety, which made no sense given that both this man and the one from the ball were strangers. She had no reason to trust strangers.

"All right, Isla, time for supper and then to bed with you."

"Must I, Papa?" The child pouted, which only made him laugh.

"One cannot conquer the world without a decent night's sleep. Isn't that right?" the man asked Sabrina the last question.

"What? Oh yes, your papa is right. Sleep is most important. Besides, the sooner you sleep, the sooner you'll be able to wake up."

The child seemed to take this into consideration and finally acquiesced. "Very well."

"Good night," he said to Sabrina, then mouthed a *thank you* before taking his girl inside.

The stew that arrived a few minutes later left much to be desired, and occasionally she would encounter something questionable with her spoon lurking in the murky depths of the bowl. But it didn't taste completely inedible, so she consumed of as much of it as she could. The single piece of bread was stale, but she used it to mop up bits of the stew.

She was still fairly hungry and decided to go down to see if they had anything else aside from stew. When she opened her door, the barmaid she'd met earlier was coming up the stairs with a plate of what looked like roast duck and potatoes, the sight of which made Sabrina's mouth water. She stopped in front of the room across the hall, and the man opened the door. "'Ere you are, my lord," the maid cooed. "Special, like you asked."

"Thank you, Mary. I am most grateful." He pressed a kiss to the hand of the maid, who turned scarlet.

"Excuse me, miss, can I order some of the duck as well?" Sabrina ventured. She didn't have much money left to spend on such a meal, but it looked too good and she was too hungry to pass it up.

The maid shot her an exasperated look. "Sorry, miss, this one is special."

"But that gentleman was able to—"

"I said it's special." The maid raised her nose at Sabrina before turning back to smile at the blond-haired man.

"Have a good night, Mary," he purred at the girl, who all but fainted before taking herself back downstairs. Sabrina looked longingly at the duck the man held on his plate.

"How did you convince her to give you that?"

The man grinned. "Oh, a bit of this, a bit of that." He winked at her and started to turn away before he stopped, sighed, and looked over at Sabrina. "Would you care to join me and my daughter? There is plenty to share."

Sabrina knew it was not a good idea to say yes, but she

was tired, hungry, and still rattled from all that had happened in the last few days.

"Oh, I shouldn't . . ."

"Nonsense. I can hear your stomach growling from here. Come inside, Miss . . ."

"Talleyrand. Sabrina Talleyrand."

"It is a pleasure to meet you. I am Rafe Lennox, and you've met my little Isla."

"Hello!" Isla piped up with a rosy-cheeked smile.

"It's a pleasure to meet you as well." She grinned at the adorable little girl as she followed Rafe into his chamber. He set the plate of roast duck down on the table, and soon the three of them were sharing a meal. She had expected Rafe to try to make some small talk, but he seemed to enjoy eating his dinner and watching his daughter in pleasant silence.

When there was no more to share, Sabrina stood and tried to offer him a few shillings.

"Please, I shall take no money, considering how I acquired the duck. It's only fitting I should share the bounty."

"Well, I thank you again, Mr. Lennox." She started back toward her room.

"Miss Talleyrand, where are you bound for, if you do not mind me asking?"

"Honestly, I am not entirely sure." She didn't mean to let herself sound so broken, but he clearly heard it in her voice.

Rafe's blue eyes seemed to glow. "Are you all right?"

"Perhaps I will be someday." She couldn't muster up the strength to put on a brave face.

"Do you have enough money to get by for now, Miss Talleyrand?"

She nodded, a pit forming in her stomach as she saw pity in his eyes.

"Well, Isla and I are bound for London. If you find yourself there and in need of assistance, you may find us on Half Moon Street, the house with the bright-blue door. You can't miss it."

"Why would you offer to help me? You do not know me."

His eyes softened, and he glanced at the child, who had somehow fallen asleep on her bed during their discussion.

"I have become more aware of the importance of helping those in need since I found Isla."

"Found?" Sabrina asked.

"Yes. She's an orphan I found in Edinburgh recently. I've taken her in as my ward, and now she is my child."

"Do you have a wife, or a governess for her?" Sabrina asked.

"I have neither. I know . . ." He laughed. "A bachelor raising a mite like her. But so far it has suited me and the child quite well."

"It is rather wonderful," she admitted. "To love a child who does not come from your blood."

"Not everyone shares that opinion."

Sabrina moved toward her room. "The world would be a better place if more did. Good night, Mr. Lennox."

"Good night, Miss Talleyrand." His voice was deep and smooth, not quite like the whiskey-rough voice of the handsome, tawny-eyed stranger from Lady Germain's ball, but she wished in that moment it was the man from the ball she'd run into in the hall. But that was only something that happened in fairy tales.

She closed the door and removed her gown before climbing into the small, cold bed and falling asleep. But her dreams were filled with glittering memories of waltzing with her mysterious stranger and making love beneath the stars.

5

Sabrina cursed softly as she studied her meager breakfast at the table down in the taproom of the inn. She had slept poorly the night before but had assured herself that anyone would have been unsettled by the strange, cold room.

The bread was even more stale this morning, hard enough to crack her teeth, and the flavorless porridge was somehow even *less* edible. She forced herself to eat as she debated where she was to go. London would provide more opportunities for work, but it would also be far more dangerous.

As the barmaid passed by, Sabrina waved her over.

"Yes, miss?"

"Excuse me, but do you know of anyone looking for any help nearby? A shopkeeper, seamstress, someone in need of a lady's maid or a milliner?" She knew her skills were lacking, but she was desperate now.

The barmaid leaned in close. "Sorry, miss, there's only a need for one sort of position around these parts, the kind you spend on your back. If you want to do that, I know a man to see about it."

"Oh, thank you, but no. I couldn't do that."

"You can if your belly stays empty long enough." The maid sniffed and walked off.

Sabrina wanted to disagree, but there was a frightening truth to that. Perhaps she had to go to London after all. By the time she collected her things and was in the stables seeing to Celeste, she already feared what the coming days would bring. She should have been worrying about the here and now.

"Well now, ain't you a pretty piece!" a gruff voice said from behind her.

Sabrina whirled to see a massive, meaty man who smelled of spirits. His bloodshot eyes were fixed on her. She held Celeste's reins, but the man blocked her path to freedom.

"Excuse me, sir, please step aside so that I may pass."

"Now, now, no need to be so 'asty," he said with a leer. "I overheard what ye were sayin' back inside. Why don't we 'ave a bit of fun, and I can send ye on yer way with a bit of coin. What d'ye say?"

She straightened herself and glared at him. "Move, or I will have my horse tread over you."

Fury lit the man's dark eyes. "So it's like that, is it?" He lunged for her, and she screeched and swung a fist at him. Celeste reared back, pulling free of Sabrina's tenuous hold on the reins. It gave the man time to grab her.

"Let go of me!"

He pulled her off her feet, and she was thrown onto a bed of hay in an empty stall. When he knelt to grab her, she savagely clawed his face.

He touched his cheek and found blood on his hand. "Oh, ye'll pay for that." He removed his belt, formed a loop, and snapped the leather against his palm. Terror overcame Sabrina as he advanced on her.

"I say—this doesn't look the least bit consenting," a voice drawled from behind her attacker. "Though I could be mistaken. Some ladies do like a bit of danger in their love life. Spices things up."

Her attacker turned to stare at Rafe Lennox, who leaned casually against a wooden beam just beyond the stall Sabrina was trapped in.

"Sod off. The bitch is mine," the man growled.

"Really, now? I had thought Miss Talleyrand had better taste." Rafe glanced at her. "Tell me, are you *consenting* to this, Miss Talleyrand?"

"To *this*? Of course I'm not consenting to this!"

"Well then, there you have it," Rafe told the man. "Off you go now."

"What?" the man huffed. "Who the 'ell do ye think ye are?"

"I am the man telling you to go. *Politely.* I may not be a saint, but I'm still a gentleman, and as such I am duty bound to intercede and free this woman from you."

"Oh, bugger off, ye puff dandy."

Rafe rolled his eyes. "I can see words are of little use here. I had better make it quick, shall I? Miss Talleyrand, please watch yourself." It was her only warning.

Sabrina scrambled back just as Rafe launched himself at the man. The flat sounds of fists striking flesh over and over and the snapping of bone made her flinch and close her eyes. The stable floor shook as the man hit the ground beside her in the stall and didn't move.

"There. It's all right, Miss Talleyrand. Our friend here is out for now," Rafe said. She opened her eyes to see Rafe holding a hand out to her. She accepted it, and he pulled her to her feet. "Perhaps when he sobers up, he'll have learned the importance of obtaining a woman's consent."

"Oh, Celeste!" Sabrina gasped.

Rafe glanced about, as though expecting to see somebody else. "Who?"

She rushed past him to grab the reins of her mare. "My horse."

"Ah, well, that's a fine bit of horseflesh," Rafe said as he joined her.

"Thank you. She was all I could take with me when I left home." She hadn't meant to say it, but it slipped out.

"And where is home?" Rafe inquired.

"It doesn't matter. Not anymore."

"Oh, so that's the way of it? Very well, we all have our secrets. Now, have you decided where you are to go?"

"London."

He offered her a grin. "Splendid. You will travel with Isla and me, then. And no, I insist upon it. Consider it your way of thanking me for saving you in such heroic fashion."

Sabrina was too tired to argue. "Thank you, Mr. Lennox. Could we tie Celeste to the back of your coach?"

"Easily arranged. My coach is ready. Now, is that your valise?" He bent to pick up her luggage.

"Yes, thank you, but I can carry it."

"You do remember I said I was a gentleman?" Rafe continued on walking, her valise secured under one arm. "This is what we do."

Sabrina followed him out of the stables, leading Celeste toward his coach. The stable lad then tied Celeste to the back of the coach. Rafe handed Sabrina's valise to the footman who was securing their luggage.

"Isla, my dear, we have a guest." A cherubic face peered out of the open coach door, and the little girl waved at Sabrina.

"Hello, Isla," she greeted as Rafe helped her inside. "Nice to see you again."

Once Sabrina was settled, Rafe sat across from her. "See, Miss Talleyrand? That was not so difficult, was it?" She stared at him in confusion, so he added, "Accepting help."

A blush reddened her cheeks. "No, my lord, it was not."

"Rafe, please. My brother is a lord, not me."

"Rafe. Then please, call me Sabrina."

"Sabrina." Rafe smiled again, and though there was the cunning of a wolf behind his smile, she did not feel threatened. Perhaps it was the adorable child next to him, but she felt she could trust him.

She spent much of the coach ride answering questions that Isla posed to her, then spoke to Rafe about all manner of topics that were very safe and quite boring.

An hour later, they reached London. When she requested to be let out on Bond Street, Rafe put a hand on the door.

"Sabrina . . . Let me ask you a question, and please know that it comes with no expectations of an amorous nature."

She tensed at the mention of the word *amorous*.

"Isla is in need of a governess. I'm new to this business of being a father, and I interviewed a dozen women in the last week, none of whom I would trust with my child. But something tells me you would do well with her. I will pay above the average rate for governesses, and I will advance your first wages to pay for a full wardrobe. I can't imagine that valise holds very much. I will also not charge room and board for you or Celeste—that will be provided in addition to your wages."

"But . . ." Sabrina tried to think of any reason to say no, and there simply was not one.

"Excellent. Now, we will proceed straight to my home, and then you will go out and purchase a wardrobe at once."

Sabrina was still stunned later that evening as she returned to Rafe's house from the modiste. She'd purchased a dozen new gowns at his insistence. Each of the gowns were serviceable and could be put on without assistance, but they were still pretty. Rafe had warned her not to return with anything drab and went so far as to threaten to burn such gowns if she did. She would have laughed, but there was a strange seriousness in his eyes as he'd replied to her giggling.

"A woman who has a profession does not have to dress so dreadfully that one forgets she is actually a person. I do not want you to blend into the bloody wallpaper. Choose colors and styles you enjoy—that is a command."

So she had, and yes, she did feel guilty about it, but she also was truly delighted. She was a governess now. She had a profession. It was safe, and she would earn her keep and her horse's. Sabrina was relieved and comforted by that thought.

Yet as she lay in bed that night, all she could do was dream about that waltz at Lady Germain's ball and all the things that had come after. What was her mystery stranger doing tonight? Was he thinking of her? Would he ever think of her, or was that one night just one of many to come with other women that he would likely forget?

"You are being silly," she chided herself. She rolled over, smashing a fist into her pillow to plump it up, and forced herself to sleep. The coming days would bring new challenges, but she needed a decent night's sleep if she was to face them.

❧ 6 ❧

E *ight months later*

PEREGRINE REMOVED HIS HAT AND COAT AND HANDED them to his butler, Jamison, as he entered his townhouse for the evening. He'd spent all day making the rounds, paying calls on families that he must now be better acquainted with. Then he'd met with his solicitors and bankers to assess all the properties and accounts that had come to him after Great-Uncle Frederick had died.

For the last eight months, he had been busy adjusting to the reality of being an earl, of having a future that lifted him out of his meager surroundings and into levels of money and power he didn't feel he had in any way earned.

"My lord, you have a letter from Mr. Lennox." His butler nodded, and a footman stepped forward with a letter on a silver tray. Peregrine was still not used to that either.

He removed the letter from the tray and went to his study. Once he was alone, he read Rafe's note. Rafe planned to visit his friend Lawrence Russell in the Cotswolds for a house party. Lawrence had apparently extended an invitation to Peregrine, since he and Peregrine were now neighbors.

Peregrine had never met Lawrence, at least not officially, but he hoped they would get on well, given that their estates bordered each other. He wrote a hasty reply directed to Rafe and then a second to Lawrence Russell, thanking him and accepting the invitation. He would need to leave in a few days to be there in time for the start of the party.

He delivered the letters to Jamison, and then he stood in the entryway of the vast empty townhouse and let out a sigh. Before his great-uncle died, he'd been living in barely tolerable lodgings in the West End of London, but at least he'd had a sense of companionship with the other people that lived nearby. Now he was utterly alone. His staff would not dare to crack a smile in his presence. He hoped that with time they would soften up, but until then, this "lordship" business was quite lonely.

"What are your plans for this evening, my lord? Should I tell the cook to have dinner ready?" The butler patiently waited for him to decide what he wished to do that night. It never ceased to amaze Peregrine how patient the man could actually be. Jamison was a bloody saint.

"I . . . well, I think I'll go out."

"Out, my lord? Should I summon your coach?"

"Yes, thank you, Jamison. I'll go to my club." At least there he would have someone to talk to.

"Yes, my lord. I'll have your coach prepared at once."

"Thank you." He returned to his study to look over some letters until Jamison summoned him.

By the time he reached Berkley's, he was surprised to find himself looking forward to an evening at the club. He'd never been a club sort of man before, even if he could have afforded it, but his need for companionship had changed that.

"Ashby?" Someone called his name as he handed his coat and hat to one of the club's footmen. Adrian Montague came down the stairs leading up to the club rooms, raising his cane in salute.

"Montague, how are you?" Peregrine asked.

He had met Adrian at a gambling hell last year, and he'd been stunned to learn the man was the bastard son of the Duke of Stratford. Adrian had spent a few years as a footman in the household of the Duke of Devon before he married Lady Venetia Dunham in a rather scandalous affair. It had been quite the event, and tongues had been wagging for months. Now, three years later, the man was happily married and father to an adorable little boy.

"It's a remarkable thing to know and be friends with two different men named Peregrine. That's why you shall always be Montague, and my other friend Sherman." Adrian chuckled at some private joke. "Although now I must get used to calling you Rutland. These bloody society rules. I can't believe it's been nearly a year since you've been titled. Damned glad to see you. I still feel at odds at a club like this, but Venetia wanted me out of the house this evening."

"Oh?" Peregrine chuckled. "Whatever for? I thought you were happily married. Did your wife toss you out?"

Adrian rolled his eyes. "I am still quite happily married, each day more than the last. But yes, she did toss me out." He grinned at Peregrine's stunned expression.

"What? Why?"

"She's hosting a surprise party for me, a birthday surprise, but the poor dear has no idea that I know what she's up to." Adrian played with the head of his cane, his lips twitching as he fought off another smile.

"How is it you know about her plans?" Peregrine and Adrian started up the stairs where they could have a drink in one of the upper rooms.

"I actually would not have had the faintest idea, she's that clever, but she has the unfortunate habit of talking in her sleep. She keeps listing things she mustn't forget to do . . . then whispering to herself about how to get me out of the house. The poor darling. I shall act all surprised when I arrive, of course. *Heavens! My darling, I had no idea!"* He raised his hands in the air and gave a mock gasp.

Peregrine burst out laughing just as they entered the main room. Several older gentlemen were asleep nearby, and one jolted awake at the sound of Peregrine's laughter.

"Hush up!" the old man grumbled before drifting back to his slumber. Adrian led Peregrine to the other end of the room where they could sit down and have a drink.

"So, how are you settling into life on the other side?" Adrian asked.

"Not very well. I thought after these last eight months, I'd be more comfortable, but I'm not." Peregrine winced at his thought of his loneliness that evening and being overwhelmed by the entire situation of taking over another man's life.

"That doesn't sound good."

"It's that damned empty house. I'm simply not used to it." Peregrine rolled his glass between his palms.

"There is one solution." Adrian motioned for one of the servers to refill his brandy.

"If you say marriage . . ." Peregrine growled in warning.

"Surely it isn't as bad as all that? Marriage surprised me. I never imagined it would be enjoyable, but here I stand . . . Or sit." He chuckled. "And I can say truthfully that it has been good for me."

"You are lucky. You do not have women after your title, tripping over themselves trying to get you to compromise them. I'm at the point of checking closets and behind curtains of any room I walk into now. It's only a matter of time before some debutante's father pops out from behind a curtain and cries *compromise* on me."

"Ah, but if you marry, you'll no longer be chased about like that." Adrian tapped his own nose as he winked. "That's how you outfox them."

Adrian's mood was infectious, and Peregrine already felt better. "You almost have me considering it, yet . . ."

"Yet what?" Adrian leaned forward. "I sense there may be a reason you are not saying that is keeping you from contemplating marriage."

"You know my views on marriage. It's a travesty inflicted upon men and women."

Adrian's jovial expression faded. "Yes, I remember you telling me about your parents, but most marriages are not unhappy, Peregrine. Even those not based on true love are often friendly alliances. You must trust that there is goodness to be had, happiness and joy to be found with the right woman. Haven't you met anyone who has tempted you to think about that?"

Peregrine was silent a long time. "There was a woman . . . last fall. I met her at Lady Germain's masquerade ball. There was something about her, something *wonderful*. She would be one I would consider, but . . ."

"But?"

"I lost her."

"How so?"

Peregrine smiled ruefully. "You will think me mad."

"Try me," Adrian said.

He told Adrian all about how he'd been at Lady Germain's ball and how a beautiful stranger had waltzed into his arms—and just as quickly out of them. He spoke of his connection with her, his desire to simply hold her, and how he'd felt an affinity for her, something that had frightened and fascinated him all at the same time.

"I may have let myself do something very foolish," Peregrine admitted.

"Such as?"

"Well . . ." He lowered his voice since he knew that it was impolite to speak of a woman in a club if he wasn't married to her. Of course, he didn't even know the woman's name, but still . . .

"We took a walk in the gardens."

Adrian lowered his voice as well. "I assume by *a walk* you mean . . ."

"Yes, and it was her wish, not mine. She told me something rather peculiar."

"During this *walk?*"

Peregrine nodded. "She claimed she was trying to avoid marriage to someone and she could only do so by disposing of her maidenhead."

"And you believed her? That is exactly what a woman would say to entrap a man in marriage."

"It occurred to me as well, but no one discovered us.

She kept her word, and neither of us removed our masks. I don't even know what she looks like."

"And you simply . . ."

"Yes, we did. And afterward, we sat together and watched the stars . . ." Peregrine sighed wistfully. He still didn't understand how that had happened. He had bedded plenty of women before he was an earl, but the peace he'd felt after being with that woman . . . He had wanted more than anything to watch the stars with her forever.

"I think you're succumbing to an incurable disease," Adrian said with a hint of a smile.

"What disease is that?"

"Love."

"Nonsense. One cannot fall in love with a stranger." Peregrine tasted his drink as his thoughts still held him in that dark starlit meadow.

"No, of course you're not in love. But you *could* be. This is proof. If you feel so strongly about her, you should find her."

"How would I do that? I cannot simply walk up to Lady Germain's house and ask for her guest list."

Adrian chuckled. "Actually, you *could* do that, but I understand your reasoning. You would have an extensive list to check. All the young ladies you would be visiting with would have marriage in mind whilst you're hunting down your erstwhile cinder princess who vanished before your eyes."

"Yes, exactly. That is what I wish above all else to avoid." Peregrine finished his drink.

"Well, then you must let this mystery woman go."

The thought made Peregrine flinch, but his friend was right. Either he summoned the courage to scour London for the woman from the ball and risk being married to another, or he let the phantom beauty go. At least then he would still have the beautiful memory of her.

"Perhaps you are right. She was a dream, not a reality, and it does me no good to dwell on dreams and not live the life set before me." Even as he said the words, part of him refused to believe them.

7

Several months ago, the first time Peregrine came to the Cotswolds, he had to keep reminding himself he was not actually a visitor, but a resident. Ashbridge Heath, the ancestral estate of the Earls of Rutland, was one of many fine properties in the area. Peregrine stepped into the foyer of his new home, still feeling like a stranger, but a welcomed one.

"We're so glad to have you back, my lord," his butler, Mr. Burton, said with a thin but honest smile.

Two butlers—one for London and one for the country.

Peregrine nearly laughed at the decadent absurdity of it all. But he was glad to be here too. He'd discovered on his first visit that the Cotswolds seemed to have a living spirit all its own, both in the people who lived and worked the land. On market days, the little village streets in the nearby towns were filled with shoppers. Then there was the sight of plows leaving rich brown ribbons of tilled earth unfurling behind them. Men and even women rode over the cresting hills and could be spotted in the distance.

It was a place of infinite variety, where dramatic changes that made the landscape behave differently only a few miles apart. What Peregrine loved most were the wild winds that swept the lonely uplands of the Cotswolds, which had grassy places where sheep scattered about and dry stone walls crossed like braids in all directions.

Unlike Peregrine's life in London before he became an earl, one that had been lived in cramped, small quarters with no real silence, he welcomed the bleak isolation of these hills and valleys. The wind whistled in a way similar to the cold air of the moors in the north of England. It was not the same as the loneliness he sometimes felt in his London townhouse. Being alone surrounded by nature was something altogether different and beautiful.

What would his mysterious stranger from so long ago think of this? He couldn't help but wonder what she would say of the landscape as he sat astride his fine bay gelding at the crest of the upper hill near his home. The spirit of the Cotswolds seemed to blow toward him up the hillside, intangible yet alive all around him. What would she think of the stars here? He knew he would be sitting outside tonight, watching the sky in a way he never had before and thinking of her.

Peregrine gave a shake of his head. He had to find a

way to banish his thoughts of that woman from his mind. He would never see her again, and that was the simple truth.

He urged his horse down the hill toward a deep wooded cleft. A sense of ancient magic and secretiveness clung to the hills and valleys here. It made him think of the stories he'd heard as a boy of King Arthur meeting with Merlin in the enchanted woods. These clefts were cold, still, and damp, yet not quite silent. If any of the old gods still slept in the world, they would be resting here, and their dreams would be a hum upon the hushed breeze that trickled through the branches and along the moss-covered stones.

Beyond the clefts were little golden villages, which created a direct and startling contrast to the hills. They were spots of seclusion, but spots full of vibrancy and warmth as well. Now that he'd visited Ashbridge a few times, he'd come to feel at home here in a way he'd never imagined possible.

This morning Burton had been extolling the virtues of the Cotswolds, and he'd told Peregrine a poem that he'd learned as a lad. It had stuck in Peregrine's mind all morning.

She was a village
Of lovely knowledge
The high roads left her aside, she was forlorn, a maid—

Water ran there, dusk hid her, she climbed four-wayed.
Brown-gold windows showed last folk not yet asleep;
Water ran, was a center of silence deep,
Fathomless deeps of pricked sky, almost fathomless
Hallowed an upward gaze in pale satin of blue.

THINKING THE WORDS MADE HIM STRANGELY HOMESICK for the home he had only just been given eight months ago. He urged his horse back toward the manor house.

Ashbridge was an old home, but it was still considered new by some standards when compared to some of the other estates in the nearby hills. It was no crumbling castle with windy corridors. Ashbridge was nestled in a remote valley at the edge of the Cotswolds. The pastures and meadowlands were enclosed by an amphitheater of steeply rising hills crowded with beech trees. The house itself was a pearl gray, surrounded by enormous yew trees, and its attendant outbuildings consisted of a church, barns, and a mill, all nestled under the lee of a steep hillside.

Burton had explained that the home was built in the Tudor era, and it had undergone some minor updates, mainly with the interior design and furnishings. Despite Great-Uncle Frederick's advancing age, he'd kept himself informed on matters of interior design. There were no dusty medieval furnishings, no threadbare bed hangings, no cracked wooden floors or faded tapestries. All in all, Peregrine had very little to do to keep himself occupied during this visit to Ashbridge Heath, so, after a few days of contemplation, he found himself looking forward to Lawrence Russell's house party.

Peregrine was nearly out of the woods when he spotted a dappled gray horse mired in a muddy bog off the side of the road. A young woman was pulling at the reins, the sounds of her sobbing and desperation immediately spurring him into action. He rode toward her and halted at a safe distance so his own horse wouldn't fall into the mud.

"Miss, may I offer my assistance?" He slid out of the saddle and set his horse to graze nearby in a field safely across the other side of the road.

She gestured to her horse, tears bright in her eyes. "Oh, please, she's trapped."

The woman wore a crimson riding habit splattered by mud, and the red riding hat she wore was perched at a jaunty angle on her dark, gleaming hair. Her face, though covered with mud, was fair, but he had seen beauty before. Yet her eyes stirred something inside him. He wanted to know everything about her at that moment, but the sound of her horse in distress jerked him back into focus.

"First things first, you must be calm. Your horse can sense your distress. That's it, dry your eyes."

She sniffed and nodded. "Yes, of course. It's only that we've been stuck here for so long, I feared I wouldn't get her out." The woman wiped at her eyes and looked between him and her horse. "I didn't see the mud until it was too late. She simply began to sink. Oh please, you must save her. I cannot bear to lose her."

"You won't. We will get her out." Peregrine studied the mud pit that had formed off the path. It looked to be no more than a foot deep, and he could easily see himself making the same dangerous mistake.

"Let me have your reins." He held out his hands, and she placed the long strips of leather into his palms. "Fetch my horse, please," he asked. While she did that, he moved closer to the bog and unfastened the bridle from her horse and looped the reins in a makeshift harness to the horse's neck and secured it to the saddle. That way, when pulled, it wouldn't strangle the horse.

She returned with his horse, and he tied the reins to the saddle of his own beast, then mounted up and began urging his horse forward. His horse pulled hard, and it gave her horse enough help to fight her way clear of the mud until the beast was standing there, panting, her sides heaving.

"Is she all right?" the woman asked.

"She should be. But give her a few minutes to recover."

Peregrine turned his attention back to the woman. Splatters of mud still flecked her cheeks. Without thinking, he removed his handkerchief and lightly dabbed at her face. He grasped her chin and continued to clean her face as she gazed innocently up at him. Her lips looked as soft as petals, and he was soon lost in a daydream of what it would be like to kiss her. He then realized what he was doing, so familiarly touching this woman whom he didn't know.

"My apologies," he stammered as he stepped back.

"It's quite all right. I must look a fright." She gestured to her mud-covered riding habit. "We were struggling for quite a while before you found us." She blushed. "My name is Sabrina . . . Talley."

"It's a pleasure to meet you, Miss Talley. I'm Peregrine Ashby." He left out his title, and the woman did not seem to recognize his name. He exhaled in relief. A woman who did not know he was an earl . . . He was tempted to further their acquaintance simply for the pleasure of her company without fear of a marriage trap. But of course, as soon as she saw where he lived . . .

"Do you live nearby?" he asked.

"No, I'm visiting. What about you?"

"I've moved here a little less than a year ago."

He suddenly had an idea. It began as a simple wishful impulse and quickly grew into something more. What if he *could* further their acquaintance without betraying that he was an earl?

"I live on the Ashbridge estate. I am the land steward there. I have a nice little cottage. You are welcome to visit me there anytime you choose." He hesitated. "I do not mean that to imply any intention of impropriety, of course. I merely could use a friend."

Sabrina smiled. "I suppose I could use a friend too. Is your home very far?" she asked.

"Not far at all," he assured her.

"Then could we have a cup of tea?"

"Yes, absolutely." He felt strangely giddy to think of this woman having tea with him. He was creating a harmless deception, all to live a life other than the grand one he'd been given by fate. Christ, Adrian would be laughing at him, if he only knew. Ever since that night at his club, when Adrian had put thoughts of love and companionship into Peregrine's head, he was seeing women in a different light. He'd always respected women, but he'd kept his distance from them when it came to any interaction that could lead to thoughts of marriage.

"Let's walk a bit. It will give your horse a chance to regain her strength." They walked side by side for a time before he said, "Forgive me, but there is something about you . . . We have not met before, have we?"

"No, it is impossible. Until last fall, I lived near Guildford."

"Have you been to London?"

"Yes, but I haven't been out much in society."

"Hmm . . ." He searched his memory for a time he might have crossed paths with her when she was in London. If he had seen her there, she would have caught his attention just as she had today, but in the crush of the London crowds, it was possible they'd passed each other without knowing.

"Which friends are you visiting? I may know them." They came into view of his home. The small steward's cottage was empty this week because Mr. Chelton was in Yorkshire looking over sheep to purchase and bring down to raise on the land.

"Perhaps you do, but I'm afraid I cannot say who." She shot him an apologetic look. "I am sorry, I'm rather cryptic, aren't I?"

"No, I apologize for prying. You may leave your horse to rest in the stables." He waved down a groom. "Timothy, I am taking Miss Talley to my cottage for tea. Please see that her horse is well cared for." He nodded meaningfully at the young man, who seemed to understand that he didn't wish to be addressed as "my lord."

"Er . . . yes, sir."

"Thank you." Peregrine then turned his attention back to Sabrina. "This way." They walked into the cozy little cottage, and he hastened to the kitchen, where he lit the stove and set a kettle on it. Years of living relatively poor had taught him some of the more basic skills that a rich aristocrat might not have.

Sabrina joined him in the kitchen and smiled. "You know how to prepare tea? Most men—"

"Are not bachelors who have learned to fend for themselves." He winked at her. "I not only boil water and steep tea, but I know quite a few other things as well."

"Well, I am impressed. My older brother grew up in much the same situation as you and fared far worse. He never quite understood that he ought to learn to care for himself once we were no longer able to afford servants."

"Let me guess, you were the one who cared for him?"

Melancholy shadowed her brown eyes, and it tugged at him, that sense that he knew her somehow. He prepared the tea, and they settled into chairs in the drawing room.

"So you work here? For the lord of the manor house?" she asked as she settled deeper into the cozy armchair. The mud was drying upon her riding habit and flaking to the floor in little patches of brown dirt at her feet. He would have to send a maid from the house to clean it up before Chelton got back.

"I do work here." Though it wasn't completely a lie, it still felt dishonest, and he hated it. But he knew that the moment she learned he was an earl, it would change everything between them. He simply wanted to be himself with at least one person.

"Do you like it? The work, I mean."

"Yes, though truth be told, there isn't much. I am not used to being so idle."

"I understand the feeling." She looked toward the small bookshelf, and her eyes lit up. "Do you enjoy reading?"

"Yes, there's no greater joy than what can be found in the pages of a good book. But don't let anyone else know I said that. Bachelors are supposed to have other hobbies, ones more prone to vices." He stood and walked over to the shelf. It was a poor quantity of books, the shelf barely half full, but he knew Chelton was a voracious reader like himself. When the steward returned from Yorkshire, he would insist the man take as many volumes from Ashbridge's library as he wished.

Sabrina removed one of the books from the shelf and flipped through the pages. Her eyes lit up with delight. "*Ivanhoe.*"

"'I have sought but a kindred spirit to share it, and I have found such in thee,'" he quoted.

Her cheeks pinkened. "My favorite was always, 'Chivalry!—why, maiden, she is the nurse of pure and high affection—the stay of the oppressed, the redresser of grievances, the curb of the power of the tyrant— Nobility were but an empty name without her, and liberty finds the best protection in her lance and her sword.'"

He gently took the tome from her as he studied it himself. "You are a reader too?"

"Yes," she admitted. "It helped to pass the time when . . ." She trailed off. "But it doesn't matter anymore."

"Why not?"

"I . . . I am hesitant to say, but seeing as you also have an occupation, surely you will not begrudge me mine."

"Begrudge you working? Of course not."

Relief softened her features. "I am a governess for a darling child."

"A worthy appointment," he said and nodded at her empty cup. "More tea?"

"Yes, please." She followed him into the kitchen, where they each prepared another cup of tea.

"You don't think it's a silly profession?" she asked.

"No, I do not. I know those who laugh at governesses, or complain about them bitterly, but it is usually not the fault of the governess for a mismatched pairing with a pupil. Most governesses are very bright women who care about their charges. It is unfair to color them any other way than courageous."

"That is such a good thing to hear," Sabrina said. "I came from a gentle-born family, but after my parents died . . . Well, my brother was not gifted in managing our wealth, nor was he clever in creating new wealth."

"Ah yes, and by virtue of birth, you, the sensible and clever child, were relegated to obeying him simply because you are female. Such nonsense. Women can be as good or as bad as men in wealth management."

"I quite agree."

"So you left your brother's home and sought your own fortune?"

"Exactly."

"I am sorry to have asked you here, then. As a gentle-born woman, surely you worry about your reputation, being seen alone with a bachelor such as me?"

"No one knows I am here, and you've been so very kind. Would you mind overmuch if I came again soon?"

"I would be glad for it, if you don't mind the risk."

Her melancholy smile tugged at him. "I do not mind. There is so little left to protect that it hardly matters."

Peregrine wondered what she meant, but he didn't ask, lest it give her more pain.

She looked toward the clock on the mantel. "Heavens, is that the time?"

"Yes, I believe so."

"Oh, I must go! I'm so very sorry!" She set her teacup down and rushed toward the door. He followed her to the stables and saw that she mounted up safely.

Then he stood in the doorway of the stables, watching her ride away. It felt as though some part of him had been tucked into the folds of her riding habit and carried away with her.

Who was Sabrina Talley? It didn't escape his notice that two women in eight months had caught his eye, and yet he knew so little of them both.

🦋 8 🦋

Sabrina was still an utter mess by the time she and Celeste arrived at Mr. Russell's country manor house. She was covered in dried splatters of mud, which would have to be washed, and she was already succumbing to her sense of guilt.

Mr. Lennox had spent a small fortune on her wardrobe when he'd first engaged her as Isla's governess, so much so that the modiste had raised a brow when she'd confirmed with her that all the gowns must also be suitable for a governess and were to be gowns that Sabrina could get into and out of without a maid's assistance. And while the wardrobe was indeed practical, the cuts and fabrics were both fine and elegant, including the dirty red velvet riding habit she currently wore.

She slipped off Celeste as she reached the stables and asked a groom to see to her.

"She fell into a mud bog, and I fear she may be injured. Will you please check her over?"

"Of course, Miss Talleyrand." The young man took Celeste's reins and gave the horse a pat on the neck, offering soothing words as he led her away.

Sabrina trudged up to the servants' entrance of the Russells' home. Servants were fluttering about belowstairs. Ever since the guests had descended on the house, such as herself and Isla and Mr. Lennox, the household had been busy. Sabrina kept out of the way as much as possible.

"Ah, Miss Talleyrand, there you are." Mrs. Benson, the Russells' housekeeper, stopped her in the hall and then blinked in surprise. "What happened, dear? Are you all right?" She touched Sabrina's shoulder in concern.

"My horse fell into a bog on the side of the road. She was stuck."

"Oh my, is she alright?"

"Yes, at least I hope so." Sabrina sighed. "A gentleman came along and rescued us." She left out the part where she had visited Mr. Ashby alone at his house.

"Well, why don't you take a bath and change? Isla will be fine in the nursery until you're ready for her."

"Thank you, Mrs. Benson."

The housekeeper squeezed her shoulder again before she left. It had surprised Sabrina to find that the staff were just as kind and welcoming as their master and mistress had been to Sabrina. That would not always be the case in other homes. Governesses were notoriously mistreated. They were neither abovestairs nor below and therefore did not belong fully to either world. She would sometimes sit with the family at dinner, but often as not she would dine with Isla, or the staff upon other occasions. She could partake in some activities, but only so long as she was tending to Isla, and since Isla was so young, it was unlikely she would spend much of her time with the adults.

After Sabrina had bathed and dressed, she found her tiny charge in the nursery.

"Miss Isla, are you ready to go outside?" she asked.

The little imp grinned and nodded, her russet curls bouncing. "Is Papa going to play with us?"

"I'm not sure, sweetheart. He has to be with the adults. But if we're lucky, he may let us join them."

"To play grown-up things?" the girl asked.

"Yes, exactly. Someday you will play them too." She hugged the girl, and Isla giggled again.

"Come on, then." She stood and clasped Isla's hand in hers. They left the nursery and climbed down the grand staircase just as Rafe was coming down the corridor.

"My darling." He knelt and opened his arms to Isla, who broke free of Sabrina's hold and rushed toward him.

Sabrina couldn't contain her smile. It had become clear over the past months she'd spent with them that Rafe truly adored his adopted child.

"How is the little scamp faring?" Rafe asked.

"Very well. We are practicing our letters, aren't we?"

Sabrina was always sure to include Isla in the conversation. The girl gave a shy but proud nod to Rafe.

"There's my girl," he praised. "A woman who reads is already in control of half the world. Isn't that right, Miss Talleyrand?"

"Yes, you are absolutely correct." Rafe had been insistent that his daughter be educated in all the ways that a boy would. No subjects were to be left out. Sabrina had to confess that she wasn't fully proficient in a few of the subjects, such as the sciences. She was doing her best to educate herself now that she had access to resources, but she worried that when the time came, Isla might need a more advanced tutor.

"Well, we're going to have a busy day. Miss Talleyrand, would you mind remaining present when Isla's with me during the party?"

She grinned at once. "Of course." It would likely be uncomfortable to be so exposed to the rest of the guests on a social level being unequal to theirs. Still, their hosts, Zehra and Lawrence Russell, had been incredibly warm and welcoming. Perhaps the other guests would be as well.

"Did you have an enjoyable ride?" Rafe asked as the three of them walked into the drawing room.

"I did, but poor Celeste became trapped in a muddy bog. I feared I might never get her out."

Rafe's cheery temperament vanished, and concern sharpened his features. "Christ, is the horse all right?"

"We're both all right. A neighbor of Mr. Russell's happened by and rescued Celeste."

"Oh? Was it Lord Rutland? He is a friend of mine. I know he enjoys riding and would likely have encountered you since his land borders Lawrence's."

"It was his steward. He was quite the gentleman."

Rafe set Isla on the settee beside him. "Oh? I haven't met the fellow."

Sabrina sat opposite them in a chair. "What does Mr. Russell have planned for today?"

"I believe once the rest of the guests arrive, it will be croquet and a picnic." He tugged one of Isla's curls. "What do you think, sweetheart? You've never been to a picnic."

"What is a picnic?" Isla asked with adorable seriousness.

"Well, let's see. A group of people sit about on some grassy hillside and admire the beautiful countryside. They eat tiny little sandwiches, perhaps a strawberry or two, and drink some punch. Then they lounge about some more. You, however, may run about to pluck wildflowers on the hillside or do whatever you wish."

"That sounds fun, doesn't it, Isla?" Sabrina asked. The girl nodded and smiled.

The drawing room door opened, and Lawrence Russell strolled in. The man was tall, with dark-red hair and hazel eyes, with the same handsomeness that had been gifted to all the Russell children. He struck a fine figure in cream-colored trousers and a dark-blue waistcoat. His wife, Zehra, had confided in her that she had been stunned by seeing so many attractive siblings in one family.

"Rafe, there you are. Rutland just arrived. I thought the three of us could oversee the preparation of the croquet wickets." When Mr. Russell caught sight of Sabrina, he offered a formal bow. "Good afternoon, Miss Talleyrand."

"Mr. Russell." She nodded at him, then held her arms open for Isla. Rafe settled Isla on her lap as he got up to join Mr. Russell.

"Would you ladies like to join us?" Mr. Russell offered to her and the child. "The weather is fine, and I imagine you would enjoy the sunshine."

"Yes, that sounds lovely."

Sabrina followed her employer and Mr. Russell into the hall, where they were speaking to another man. She drew closer, then jerked to a stop as she recognized him. Mr. Ashby, the man who had rescued her beloved horse and had given her such an enjoyable morning. Only a short time ago she'd been alone with him, discussing literature in a cozy little cottage. He was just as gorgeous as she'd believed a few hours ago. She licked her lips as she suddenly realized she was parched. His tawny eyes flicked to hers, widening in shock, then flaring in pleasure as he spoke.

"Sabrina?"

Her mind spun with excitement and then panic as she

realized he'd called her by her Christian name in front of her employer.

"Mr. Ashby . . ." She tried desperately to put a barrier between them since her employer was now staring between the two of them.

"You know my governess, Peregrine?" Rafe asked in surprise.

"Yes," he said slowly. "I met her this morning."

"This is the man I told you about, sir. The man who saved Celeste from the mud bog," Sabrina supplied quickly.

Rafe's glance moved swiftly between her and Mr. Ashby. She could almost see him putting pieces together.

"But I thought you said that the man who aided you was a land steward. Ashby is no steward. He's the *Earl* of Rutland."

For a second she didn't understand what Rafe had said, and then his words sank in and she hastily sought to cover her sudden shock. He must have concealed his title for a reason, and while she was upset at his deception, she would not call him out on it in front of the others.

"I . . . I must've been mistaken," she said. She felt Isla press against her side, her tiny hand tightening around Sabrina's.

Sabrina shifted on her feet uneasily. All she wanted right then was to avoid scandal in whatever form it came in. Mr. Ashby—Lord Rutland, for that was how she must think of him now—had lied, but she wasn't sure why, and she was in no position to demand the truth from him. She dug the nails of her free hand into her palm, the slight pain bringing her some much-needed focus.

"The fault is mine," Rutland said at last. "I did not introduce myself properly."

Properly? The word echoed in Sabrina's head as her confusion began to turn to anger. He had *lied* to her about who he was, and he was not explaining why. He had told her that he was a steward, that he *worked* for the earl. Yet here he was, the Earl of Rutland. Why had he lied to her, and why was he *still* lying in front of Rafe and Mr. Russell?

For a moment, she and Rutland stared at each other. Rafe coughed, and she broke off her gaze, looking to the floor.

"Well, now you've met properly," Rafe said. "Shall we go?"

Lord Rutland was still staring at her, a strange expression on his face.

"Come along, Peregrine. We have to see to the wickets." Rafe nudged the earl none too gently in the ribs. Rutland blinked, as though dragging himself out of his thoughts, and then shot Rafe a scowl.

Sabrina and Isla stayed a good distance behind the three gentlemen as they strode ahead. When they reached a grassy lawn, two footmen were waiting with a dozen wickets in their hands.

"Let's sit and watch," Sabrina told Isla as they paused before a bench. She helped the child sit down on the bench beside her so they could observe the men. From the start, it was clear Lord Rutland and Mr. Russell wanted a fair game, but Rafe was determined to arrange the wickets so it would be nearly impossible in several places to strike a ball through them. A fairly energetic argument broke out, and suddenly the three men were throwing wickets at each other and running about shouting like wild boys. Sabrina laughed at the immature sight.

Zehra Russell came to stand beside Sabrina and Isla's bench. "Heavens, they never truly grow up, do they?"

"No, they never do." Sabrina moved over on the bench and set Isla on her lap so Zehra could sit down beside them. Lawrence Russell's wife was beautiful and had an interesting past. Rafe had told her that Zehra's father was a Persian prince and her mother the daughter of an English duke. With exotic eyes and the dark-gold tint of her skin, Zehra was blooming here in the Cotswolds.

"How are you settling in, Sabrina?" she asked.

"Quite well. I cannot thank you and your husband enough for letting me stay here."

"Of course." Zehra smiled at her before looking back at the men.

"Zehra . . . what do you know of Lord Rutland?"

It was a risk to ask such a probing question, but she felt deep in her bones that she could trust Zehra with any inquiries that might reveal her interest in the earl.

"Not much, I'm afraid. He is a friend of Rafe's. I believe he's only been an earl since last fall." Zehra covered her laugh with a hand as Mr. Russell grabbed Rafe, one arm around the back of his neck, so that Rafe was trapped beneath Russell's armpit as he tried to wrestle him to the ground.

"Have Rafe and Mr. Russell known each other a long time?" Sabrina asked.

Zehra nodded. "Since they were young men. Their older brothers became acquainted at university and, well, the rest is history."

"History?"

"Yes, you know, the League of Rogues. Their brothers are both members," Zehra explained, but then her eyes widened in shock. "You don't know who they are?"

Sabrina shook her head. "Are they famous?"

Zehra smiled. "More like *infamous*. There were five of them, originally—a duke, an earl, a baron, a marquess, and a viscount. They were all notorious bachelors until they made one mistake."

"What was that?" Sabrina was already drawn into her story.

"They kidnapped a woman named Emily. It was revenge, you see, because her uncle had stolen from the duke, but that's what started it all. That one woman brought the five men to their knees, and now they are all happily married. Now it seems it is starting to trickle down to their brothers. I believe Lawrence never knew how lonely he was until Lucien got married. Men are far more social creatures than they dare ever admit." Zehra gave her a soft smile. "And they can be unbearably romantic and sweet too."

Sabrina thought of her masked stranger and how they had made love beneath the stars. He could have so easily gotten up and returned to the ball after satisfying his own lust, but he'd stayed and reached for her hand and held it as they watched the sky. That had been romantic. He would never know what that had meant to her, to hold on to her when she'd been so at risk of drifting away.

"My dear, Rafe's face is turning blue. Best to let him breathe!" Zehra called out, snapping Sabrina out of the memory. Mr. Russell released Rafe, who promptly walloped him in the stomach. The Earl of Rutland watched this boyish play unfold with a bemused grin. Then he turned away and came toward her, Zehra, and Isla.

Zehra stood and held out her hands to the little girl. "Isla, come with me, my darling. Why don't we go tackle your papa to the ground?"

Isla squealed in delight and rushed at her father. Rafe fell to the ground and begged for mercy as his daughter climbed all over him. Zehra stood by her husband, watching Rafe and Isla with a fondness that made Sabrina's heart swell.

"May I sit?" Rutland asked.

"Of course, my lord." She didn't want to look at this handsome man, even when he spoke. She was still angry. Yet she couldn't deny that her body buzzed with him sitting so close. He rested his hand on the bench, the edge of his palm just grazing the fabric of her gown. She tried stubbornly to ignore him. They were two people sitting on a bench. That was all. They did not need to say a thing to each other.

"I'm sorry I did not tell you who I really was. I was unprepared to share my title. I've seen far too many women change around an unmarried man with a title, money, and lands." He sighed, the sound heavy.

She'd been so determined not to look at him, but that sound was one she recognized. She understood that weariness that weighed upon a person's soul. But she wouldn't create excuses for him.

"Are you boasting about yourself, my lord, or are you insulting me?" she asked quietly, raising her chin as she pinned him with what she hoped was a regal glare.

He flinched. "Neither of those. Actually, I'm lodging a complaint. I have not been the Earl of Rutland very long. To myself, I'm still Peregrine Ashby."

Sabrina did look at him then, and what she saw filled her with a dark, wild longing. This dark-haired man with tawny eyes reminded her of a bird of prey, strong, fast, intelligent, yet she didn't fear him.

"Then I must admit that I am Miss Talleyrand, not Talley. I, too, was trying to hide a little." She wanted to trust him, but in the past she'd mistrusted people and been proven a fool. Her brother hadn't even searched for her after she'd fled his home that awful day. She was both relieved and hurt to not even be missed. But it was a chapter she'd closed in the book that was her life.

Peregrine studied her. "Why do you wish to hide?"

She shrugged. "My life has changed, and I am no longer in the station I once was."

"You shouldn't be ashamed of anything. Before last fall, I was barely above a pauper, making only small bits of money at gambling establishments. And unlike many men, I gambled out of desperation rather than pleasure. I'm not proud of it, but I can be honest about it." He held out an arm. "Walk with me?"

She found herself placing her hand on his arm. "You aren't ashamed to walk about before your friends with a governess?" she asked.

He grinned. "I've done far more scandalous things in my life than walk with a lovely young woman."

They moved away from the croquet lawn into the gardens. Sabrina couldn't help but feel something strange come over her, a sense of déjà vu.

"This may sound rather silly, but I feel as if I've done this before," she admitted.

Peregrine tilted his head. "Walked in the gardens?"

"Yes—well, no. Oh, never mind. Please forget I mentioned it." She didn't want him thinking any less of her by what she really meant.

"Would you tell me about Ashbridge?" she asked. "Now that I know the entire estate is your home, I should like to hear about it."

At this Peregrine smiled. "It is a large property, and I've only been able to acquaint myself with it a few times over the last eight months, but I rather like the place. My butler tells me that later in the spring, when all the flowers are blooming, it will be quite a sight. It should be but another month before we see those glorious colors."

"I should like to see that. It's a pity that I won't be here."

"Perhaps I shall invite Rafe to come directly to my home after this party. He would surely bring the child, which will therefore make him bring you as well."

Sabrina dared not hold out much hope that that would happen. Peregrine was an eligible bachelor of thirty with money, lands, and a title. By his own account he was the subject of many husband-hunting women, and it was foolish for her to entertain any thoughts that he might be truly interested in her in any other way than a platonic one.

She pulled free of his arm and walked a bit on her own before turning back to face him. A strange thing happened. In that instant, Peregrine was gone, and she saw a man in a mask standing beneath a starlit sky. She banished the memory. It was too eerie to think of Peregrine and the man in the garden. They *weren't* the same man, yet she wanted to pretend in her heart of hearts that he was.

Zehra had spoken of loneliness and men, but women

fell prey to such agonies as lonely hearts too. And right then, she felt so very lonely.

"Miss Talleyrand . . . ," Peregrine began, then he shook his head before he hurried to catch up with her as they exited the gardens.

Sabrina returned to Isla and he to his friends. They were doing what they should. Staying apart. An earl and a governess had no need to be together in any way, no matter how she might wish it were possible.

❧ 9 ❧

"Rafe, how did you meet Miss Talleyrand?" Peregrine asked as he watched the other man line up his shot for the tenth wicket. The final guests for the week-long party had arrived in the last hour, and a good number of ladies and gentlemen had gathered near the croquet lawn, mallets in their hands. The light breeze tugged on the skirts of the ladies, making them look like a flock of colorful birds gracefully moving about the gardens.

"How did I meet Sabrina?" Rafe swung and with a solid *whack!* the ball ripped through the wicket and bounded down part of the small slope to the rest of the lawn below.

"Yes, Sabrina. How did you meet her?"

"I came across her at an inn when Isla and I were returning to London shortly after Lady Germain's party last fall. She was without any money and had no clothes but those upon her back. A man attacked her in the stables, I intervened, and she agreed to accept my offer of employment as a governess." Rafe was watching Peregrine closely. "Why are you interested?"

Peregrine tried to feign indifference. "There is a sadness about her. It lends her an air of mystery that has me a bit curious."

Rafe chuckled. "A bit curious? You, the man who vows not to marry until he must is now interested in a woman who *deserves* marriage."

"I am not thinking of marriage," Peregrine admitted, feeling foolish.

"Normally, I would encourage a man to sow his wild oats and whatnot, but not with *my* governess. I like her, and Isla likes her. I will not have you swoop in and seduce her just to have some dalliance."

"First, I am not a man to swoop," Peregrine replied coldly. "And I would not seduce her. I'm merely curious."

"So you've said." Rafe sounded entirely unconvinced as he watched Peregrine with a level of scrutiny he didn't at all like.

Peregrine took his turn. Right before he hit the ball, he glanced toward where Sabrina stood with a few of the ladies. They were talking, and Isla stood close to her, one hand curled in the woman's skirts. Sabrina looked stunning in a light-gray satin gown with pale rosebuds embroidered on the bodice and the gown's hem. She looked even more quietly elegant than the women around her.

"So have you had time to settle into your life as an earl?" Rafe broke into his thoughts.

"Yes, a little, but not nearly as much as I had hoped I would." He whacked his ball, and it skittered wildly across the grass, striking the Earl of Lonsdale's foot.

"Oi, watch it, Rutland!" he barked and kicked the croquet ball away from his boot. Several ladies and gentlemen cried foul at the disruption of the game, but Lord Lonsdale told them all to sod off.

When Peregrine glanced back at Sabrina, she had a gloved hand over her mouth, trying to hide the grin on her face. Peregrine grinned back at her.

"You had better put your eyes back in your head, man, and look elsewhere for fun," Rafe warned.

Peregrine tried. He did everything a gentleman ought to do to distract himself from focusing too much on a lady. But it was no use. He couldn't get past that sadness he'd seen in her, and he wished to do something to make amends for his earlier deception. He made a hasty trip back to Ashbridge and pored over the library books before he'd selected a few to give to her tonight—under the guise of friendship, of course. That evening, he maneuvered himself into escorting her from the drawing room to the dining room when all the guests were ready for dinner.

"My lord," she greeted him as he held out his arm. His heart gave a wild jolt as she placed her hand on his forearm, giving him the excuse of pulling her closer to him.

He leaned in a little, his head tilted toward hers as they began to walk toward the dining room. "Miss Talleyrand." She smelled of wildflowers, a scent that called upon his memory, demanding that he remember something that kept eluding him.

He pushed her seat in and then claimed the chair next to hers. The table was large. Fifteen people were in attendance, which gave him time to speak with Sabrina.

"I brought some books from my library for you. I thought perhaps you might like them."

"Oh?" Her brown eyes brightened.

"Yes, some medieval poetry, which I assure you is far more interesting than it sounds, and some rather excellent editions of Sir Walter Scott, including *Ivanhoe*."

"Thank you, my lord, I would be quite interested," Sabrina murmured around the edge of her wineglass.

Peregrine focused on her lips, such a soft pink, like the petals of a budding rose. It was a color that spoke of life to come, of kisses still on the horizon, of whispers yet to be shared, and sweet sighs that gave a man the most pleasant dreams.

"You're staring," the woman on his other side said in a low voice.

Peregrine turned his focus to Lysandra Russell, Lawrence's little sister. She was an eccentric creature, as beautiful as she was intelligent, with dark-red hair and warm hazel eyes that sparked with irritation when she spoke to someone who could not keep up with the fast pace of her mind.

"What?"

"You are staring at the governess. People are bound to notice."

"She isn't just a governess," he muttered back.

"Of course not. All women are more than one simple thing," Lysandra replied. "But you had best be careful. If you keep staring, it will make her uncomfortable."

This bit of reasoning got through to him. The last thing he wanted was to upset Sabrina, when he knew how worried she was about her status. He refocused his gaze on the food courses and politely chimed in when spoken to. But when he had the chance, he still hoped to speak to Sabrina. After dinner, he escorted her into the drawing room with the other guests.

"I should retire," she said to him. "Isla is asleep."

"Please stay," he begged.

She lingered in the corner of the room. One of the women began to sing while someone played the pianoforte. Rafe suddenly called out to Peregrine.

"Rutland, you enjoy poetry—come recite something."

Peregrine shot Rafe a stoic look. "I don't have anything prepared."

"Surely you have a classic memorized—all good gentlemen do," Rafe replied. The entire room watched the two men have a momentary battle of gazes.

"Why is he forcing you to recite poetry?" Sabrina asked in a whisper.

"Because the damned fool has some idiotic notion that I will seduce you away from him and Isla. This is his way of keeping us apart."

Sabrina let out a soft gasp, which drew his focus to the flush of color now present in her face.

"I really should go, then. I mustn't upset Mr. Lennox." She started to leave, but Peregrine risked Rafe's wrath by gently taking her hand.

"Stay for my dreaded poetry recital?" he asked.

Her gaze dropped to his hand, and a flush of pink crept up her cheeks like slow-blooming flowers. She seemed to debate with herself whether to accept his strange invitation.

"Very well," she sighed. He caught a glimmer of something else in her eyes, but he dared not give it a name.

"Rutland, *now*, if you please," Rafe called out.

With great reluctance, he left Sabrina to stand at the front of the drawing room, where everyone had gathered on chairs and settees to listen. Peregrine tried to erase the glower from his face and schooled his features as he prepared himself.

At first he didn't stare at her, but instead at the back of the room, as he'd done when he'd been a young man, forced to recite verses in the schoolroom. But soon his gaze drifted toward her, her magnetism too strong to resist.

For weal or woe I will not flee
To love that heart that loveth me.

That heart my heart hath in such grace
That of two hearts one heart make we;
That heart hath brought my heart in case
To love that heart that loveth me.

For one the like unto that heart
Never was, nor is, nor never shall be,
Nor never like cause set this apart
To love that heart that loveth me.

Which cause giveth cause to me and mine
To serve that heart of sovereignty,
And still to sing this latter line:
To love that heart that loveth me.

Whatever I say, whatever I sing,
Whatever I do, that heart shall see
That I shall serve with heart loving
That loving heart that loveth me.

This knot thus knit, who shall untwine,
Since we that knit it do agree
To loose not nor slip, but both incline
To love that heart that loveth me?

Farewell, of hearts that heart most fine,
Farewell, dear heart, heartly to thee,
And keep this heart of mine for thine
As heart for heart, for loving me.

AS HE SPOKE THE LAST FEW LINES, IT SEEMED AS THOUGH only he and Sabrina were left in the room together. Something powerful was building between them, and the flush of her skin matched the warmth of his own.

There was a long moment of silence before Zehra spoke up. "My lord, that was lovely." The other women were all in agreement, though most of the gentlemen looked bored. Lord Lonsdale was already asleep in a chair, and one of the ladies nearest him prodded him into waking up. He shook himself and realized Peregrine had finished.

"I say, well done, Rutland. Didn't know you could sing like that. Excellent voice." Lonsdale clapped a few times, and a few of the women stifled giggles.

"Charles," Lysandra hissed. "He didn't sing—he recited poetry."

"Oh, right." Lonsdale looked back at Peregrine with a sardonic smile and a shrug. Peregrine sighed. When he looked back toward the corner of the room, he found Sabrina had gone. His heart sank. She hadn't stayed. He thought of the books he wanted to give to her. He could not chase her down now—everyone would know they were gone, and that would only put her reputation more at risk.

SABRINA LAY AWAKE IN HER BED, THINKING OVER THE poem that Peregrine had recited. It was old, perhaps even medieval. She had liked it immensely, and the gentle rhythm as he'd spoken the words had soothed something still wounded inside her. After all these months, she still felt part of herself was missing. She just wasn't sure what it was.

She quickly banished thoughts of it and him, or at

least she *tried* to. Rafe did not want her meeting with any gentlemen, and she shouldn't. This was not a social visit. It was her employment, to be here and to see to Isla, not to enjoy herself. She owed it to Rafe to be the governess he needed for Isla.

However, she still could not sleep after midnight and decided she would go down to the kitchens for a glass of milk to see if that might calm her. She pulled on her robe and slipped out of bed. The stone floor was icy, so she slipped into a pair of silver mule slippers and began the long walk from her bedchamber to the kitchens. She descended the main stairs, and the boisterous sounds of men laughing still came from the billiard room. Why men would stay awake so late she would never know.

Once in the darkened kitchens, it took her a moment to light a few candles before she found a saucepan and began to warm some milk. She was pouring it into a glass when she heard booted steps outside the open door.

Peregrine stood there, looking more a handsome man of leisure than ever in buckskin trousers and a white lawn shirt. His crimson-colored waistcoat, patterned with gold-embroidered stag heads, accented his broad chest all the way down to his narrow hips, giving him a fine masculine figure. For a second she froze, too entranced by the sight of him to remember that she was to avoid being alone with him. The faint sound of the men carousing above them echoed down the stairs, but it faded away the longer she stared at him.

"Miss Talleyrand—I'm sorry, I—" He cleared his throat. "What are you doing down here?"

"I thought a bit of milk would help me sleep." She stepped to the side so he could see the saucepan.

"Oh, yes. As it happens, I'm here for that as well."

"Milk?"

He nodded. "And for those." He grinned bashfully and pointed at the plate of strawberry tarts nearby. "I have a sudden urge for sweets."

She smiled back. "Me too."

"Would you like one?"

"Do you suppose the cook will be mad if she finds them missing tomorrow?" Sabrina asked.

"If she is, we'll blame Lonsdale and Rafe for it. Agreed?" He held out a hand.

With a laugh, she accepted and shook it. She poured more milk into the saucepan and warmed a second glass while Peregrine put two tarts on a pair of plates. They carried their milk and secret dessert out of the kitchen.

"To the library?" Peregrine suggested.

"You don't think anyone will be there?"

"At this hour? Christ, no. Only the men are still awake, and I can promise you not one of them will be in the library."

"Won't they know you've gone?"

"They know, and they don't expect me back. I told them I was off to bed, and I was, before I decided I needed something sweet."

She wished she could find an excuse to go straight up to bed herself, but in truth she didn't want to. She wanted to see him again. There was something about him that calmed her and yet strangely excited her.

"Very well, direct me to the library."

Once they arrived, they settled into two chairs by the fire.

"This is rather nice, isn't it?" he asked as they enjoyed their desserts.

"It is," she agreed. "Lord Rutland, I must tell you I enjoyed that poem you recited this evening." She couldn't help but steal a glance at him and noticed he was doing the same toward her.

"I thought you'd left," he said.

"No, I stayed until the moment you finished, and then while everyone was distracted by Lord Lonsdale I slipped out. Your poem was beautiful."

"Thank you. I admit I did feel rather inspired to choose that one."

They were silent a long moment before Sabrina spoke. "My lord . . ."

"Peregrine, please. I should like us to be friends. Everything I said in my steward's cottage was the truth. Only my title was hidden from you." He gazed earnestly at her, and she was struck again by his handsome features and how they accompanied a tender and gentle heart to match.

This man was no heartless rake, but someone like her,

whose circumstances had changed unexpectedly. In another life, she would have wished to marry a man like him, but she had dropped in the ranks of society and he had risen, and now the disparity was too great between them.

"I would like to be friends as well," she finally said and bit into her tart again, savoring the last bite of its sugary sweetness. She set the plate on a nearby table, knowing that a maid would put it away in the morning. She remained silent as he finished his, searching for what to say. She had a thousand things she wanted to discuss with him, knowing their conversation could flow so easily, but she dared not keep herself in this position much longer and risk being discovered.

"I should go to bed now." She stood, and he hastened to his feet as well.

"I still have those books . . . Please allow me give them to you. Stay here, and I shall return with them in a moment."

She waited, still in her nightgown and robe by the fire, the taste of sugar on her lips as she thought of how very dangerous this was. Ever since that night at the masked ball, she knew what could happen between men and women in the dark when passion burned between them. It would be only too easy to let herself go with Peregrine, just as she had with the man at the ball. Each time she was near him, she was haunted by bittersweet memories of that starlit night.

Realizing she'd made a mistake in waiting for him, she started toward the library door to return to her bed, but he suddenly returned, his arms wrapped around a stack of books. He set them on the table and lifted the top one. It was an old text, one that reminded her of Chaucer's *Canterbury Tales*. He opened it to one of the early pages.

"This book contains the poem I read tonight."

She scanned the text. "But this is in Middle English. You didn't recite in that form tonight."

"No, I am sadly familiar with Middle English. I learned it at university in order to prove one of my professors wrong." He crossed his arms and leaned back against the edge of the reading table, his long, lean muscled legs outlined in those buff breaches. For a second Sabrina found herself distracted by his body and not his mind.

"Heavens, Middle English—even I did not enjoy learning that. However did you manage it?"

"It was like having a tooth pulled, or a shoulder set back into place. I rather hope to never experience anything like that again." He moved closer to her, his shoulder touching hers innocently as she read a few of the poems. Heat sizzled along her upper arm where they connected, and she trembled.

"Are you cold?" He put an arm around her shoulders. His scent enveloped her as he pulled her closer, a scent she realized she knew only too well. Sandalwood and leather. Was she dreaming? This couldn't be . . . Could it? Her head spun at the thought that this man might actually be the one who appeared in so many of her dreams. But it had been so many months, she had to admit she could be mistaken.

"I'm not cold," she whispered.

He gazed down at her now, his eyes inviting and warm as he licked his lips.

This was wrong. She shouldn't do this . . .

She *wanted* to do this.

And so, in keeping with a lifetime of poor decisions, she leaned in and turned her face toward him just as he bent his head toward her. Their heads collided with a sharp *crack!* He groaned and clutched his forehead, and at the same time she held a hand to her own and gave a little yelp.

"Bloody hell," he muttered. "I'm so sorry, Miss Talleyrand."

"No, no, I'm sorry," she said with a sigh full of regret. That little blunder had cleared her head. She should not go about kissing anyone. That part of her life had been over before it had ever begun.

"Here, let me see." He caught her chin and turned her face toward him. He gently examined her forehead. "Not even a red spot. Does it hurt?"

"Not very much," she admitted. "Mostly my pride. You?"

"Not at all now." He was still holding her chin in his hand. "Please let me try that again," he said with a gentle twinkle in his eyes.

"What about our agreement to be friends?" she asked, tilting her face up. How could this man make her so hopelessly full of dangerous desire?

"I never agreed to only be friends. I said that I would not seduce you. You are seducing *me*, if truth be told. I'm quite powerless in your hands, Miss Talleyrand."

"Sabrina, please." She needed him to say her name. She wanted to let her fantasies run away with her, that he was indeed her mystery man who'd saved her and given her something magical that she would never forget. A night of love beneath the stars . . .

"Sabrina," he whispered her name in that husky voice potent with yearning and midnight hunger.

Then he kissed her, and it was everything she had hoped it would be. Peregrine wrapped one arm around her waist, pulling her flush against him, and she sighed in delight against his mouth.

"Open your lips for me," he said.

She trembled in his arms. It had to be him, her masked mystery man from Lady Germain's ball. She did as she had that night and parted her lips. He cupped the back of her head, and his hand threaded through her loose hair until he pulled on the strands just enough to let her feel how in control he was at the moment, but she wasn't afraid. She felt protected and cherished with him, just as she had that night at the ball.

She curled her arms around his neck, holding him close as she gave in to her building desires. It merged with her longing for the masked man she had seduced at the ball until it became this one *perfect* moment.

I really am the seducer.

The thought made her giggle a little as their lips broke apart. He grinned down at her, seeing her amusement.

"What is it?" he asked. His fingers massaged the back of her neck, removing the last bit of tension in her muscles.

"It's nothing. Please don't stop kissing me." She pulled his head back down to hers.

They stayed like that for a long while, kissing by the firelight until she thought she might forget her very self and never leave that room or his embrace again.

He lifted her up onto the nearest reading table, putting her mouth at a closer height to his own. She gasped as he slid his hands up her thighs, pushing her skirts up to her hips so he could step between her spread legs. Then he dragged her closer to him, pressing her body tightly to his own. The hardness of his arousal pressed against her core, but he didn't claim her. He simply kissed her and held her, his hands roving and exploring her thoroughly.

"Peregrine," she whispered against his lips.

"Yes?"

"Please touch me . . ." She wanted his hand between her legs. She knew what pleasure could come from his touch, and she craved it so madly that she thought she would die if he refused her.

"Touch you?" He slid his hand down her side, brushing

his palm over the curve of her hip until he reached between her legs. "Like this?" he asked, his voice rough with passion as he traced a fingertip around her wet folds.

"Yes, there!"

He didn't hesitate. He entered her with that finger, gentle at first, then more firmly until she was pushing to get closer. His mouth on her lips was hard now, hungry and almost violent in a way that made her feel wild. There was no worry outside of this moment, no concern for tomorrow. There was only him touching her, him kissing her . . .

The climax caught her so suddenly that she cried out. He drowned the sound with his lips over hers, and she melted into him, boneless and free. He held her, still kissing her, but his lips softened into sweet, fluttering presses that made her heart quiver.

"You are beautiful when you come apart," he whispered in her ear. He kissed her temple and held her as her trembling aftershocks faded. There were a thousand things she wanted to say to him, yet she could say not one.

By the time she crawled into bed, her arms full of books he had brought her, she was grinning like a fool, her heart warm and her mind dizzy. She was certain she had found her mystery lover, but she could never tell him. All she could do was enjoy what time she had left with him before they parted ways again.

She decided she would take a chance, let herself enjoy this small pleasure while she could. It was not as though she had a future marriage to worry about. As long as she didn't allow it to interfere with her minding of Isla or bring scandal to Rafe, she could have some passion before surrendering to a loveless life.

Tonight, she would only think of Peregrine and the way the fire had lit up his tawny eyes, so like the falcon for which he was named, and how she had been completely and utterly lost in them.

10

At luncheon, Peregrine was still grinning like an idiot at the dining room table. Last night had been wonderful. Sitting and talking with Sabrina, holding her in his arms, he had felt like he was back at Lady Germain's again. Somehow lightning had managed to strike twice. He hadn't thought it possible to feel the same unimaginable passion with another woman after he'd made love to that mysterious fae queen beneath the stars.

Yet Sabrina had brought that feeling of magic back to him. That was what he'd been missing in life these last several months. The aching loneliness he felt as the Earl of Rutland had not only been tempered but was fading the more he thought of Sabrina.

"Had your fill of canaries, have we?" Rafe asked as Peregrine filled his plate with food.

Peregrine sat down across from Rafe. "Canaries?"

"You look like a satisfied tomcat who's eaten a few too many plump little birds."

Peregrine's good humor waned a bit. "No, I slept well for the first time in months, that's all."

Rafe gave an unconvinced harrumph. "Well, you'd be wise to stay on your best behavior," he reminded him.

The door to the dining room opened, and a stream of ladies came in. The last to enter was Sabrina, who held Isla by the hand. Peregrine stared at the lovely green gown she wore, gathered at the back by a dark-blue satin sash. The gown itself was the shade of summer grass on a perfectly manicured lawn. Her dark hair was pulled back with a ribbon at the base of her neck rather than pulled up in the current style. She led Isla over to a chair beside Rafe, then sat on Isla's other side.

"Afternoon, my darling." Rafe chucked his daughter under the chin, his open smile clearly full of love for his child.

"Good afternoon, Papa." Isla greeted him with a grin as big as her father's.

"We are to have a scavenger hunt this afternoon," Zehra announced when the last of the guests arrived in the dining room for lunch. Several of the men at the table grumbled, and Lawrence stood up.

"Now, now, we're going to make it interesting. First, there will be random pairings. I will put all of our names upon slips of paper and draw them out of a bowl. The winners will be awarded a new colt from Viscount Sheridan's stables. A thoroughbred born by one of his Arabian mares. She had twins, and he was gracious enough to offer one of them to the winners. I will send word to him in London naming the lucky pair. The winning pair can work out the ownership of the foal between them."

At this announcement, every man at the table suddenly sat up, including Rafe.

Lonsdale grinned. "Well now, this changes things. I've only been trying for years to get Cedric to sell me a horse, and here he is just *gifting* one away." Lonsdale pushed his empty plate away and stood. "Well, on with it. Pair us up and let's get started!"

Lawrence chuckled as Zehra handed him a bit of paper. He scrawled down the names of everyone at the table, then tore the paper into strips. He folded up each name and put them in a white-and-blue china bowl. He swirled the names about with his fingers in an overly dramatic fashion. Both Lonsdale and Rafe looked ready to knock Lawrence down and pull the names out themselves. Peregrine tried not to laugh. When Lawrence finally began to speak, the entire room went silent.

"Zehra, you are with"—Lawrence dug for a second name—"Alexandra."

Zehra smiled at her partner, the wife of Ambrose Worthing, a man Peregrine had only met yesterday but had immediately liked.

"Next, Rafe, you'll be with . . . Darlington."

Rafe exchanged a cunning grin with Vaughn Darlington, who sat at the end of the table next to his wife, Perdita. The viscount had once been quite a wicked man, if one believed the gossip, but his marriage of convenience to Perdita had ended up a romantic love match.

Rafe and Darlington would be a dangerous pair. Peregrine knew they were both clever men.

"Let's see . . . Next up, me." Lawrence set his name down on the table. "And I'm with Gareth." He nodded at Gareth Fairfax, a quiet but respectful man in his midthirties who was absolutely mad for his sweet and vibrant wife, Helen. Peregrine had been enjoying meeting these new sets of couples. There was not one among them he wouldn't be proud to call his friends.

"Helen, you are with Ambrose." Lawrence sloshed the remaining names around in the bowl. "And Linus, you will be with Perdita."

Linus, Lawrence's youngest brother, smiled shyly at Vaughan's dark-haired wife.

"Who's left?" Lawrence asked as he glanced around the table.

"Me, damn you," Lonsdale said.

Lawrence laughed again. "Charles, you are with . . . oh . . . Lysandra."

Lonsdale grinned wickedly at Rafe. "Well, well, Rafe. I got the smartest person in the room as my partner. Isn't that right, Lysa?" Lonsdale shot a charming smile at Lysandra. The young woman blushed.

"She may be the smartest, but she still has you to deal with," Rafe shot back. "Call it a handicap."

"So that puts Miss Talleyrand with Rutland," Lawrence finished, ignoring Rafe and Lonsdale's verbal sparring.

Peregrine couldn't believe his luck. He'd been paired with Sabrina. He schooled his features so as to hide his excitement, though thankfully Rafe was preoccupied with his quarrel with Lonsdale.

"Let's make this interesting," Rafe said to Lonsdale. "Hundred pounds to the winning pair."

"Done." Lonsdale shook hands with Rafe.

Lawrence spoke up. "All right, Zehra has clues for each pair. They've been prepared by our butler, who has a knack for this sort of thing. You have two hours. Whoever finds the final clue will be declared the winners."

Peregrine's heart raced as he and Sabrina exchanged glances. He had a sanctioned two hours to spend with her, and Rafe could say nothing about it.

Everyone paired up, and Zehra passed out the first clue. The rest of the clues were located at hidden spots, leading up to the final clue. When they discovered one, they were to read it and then place the clue back where they had found it.

Sabrina received the paper with their copy of the first clue. She and Peregrine, along with little Isla, went over to the window to read it in better light. Peregrine lifted Isla up on a chair near them so she could see the paper, even though she was still learning to read.

"Clue number one," Sabrina read softly.

Do not frown at me, I made it clear.

It won't make a difference if you're near.

Stand in front of me beneath the starlight,

And I'll show you exactly how the world will know you.

Peregrine repeated the words under his breath. "*Starlight* . . . Well, it isn't night and won't be before the challenge is done, so it must be something else."

"Yes, my thoughts exactly," Sabrina agreed. "And it must be something you stand in front of . . . The fireplace?"

Peregrine automatically glanced around the dining room. The other pairs had already departed. They were alone, and the fireplace was there opposite them.

"But fire does not make anything clear. It burns and the smoke obscures."

"Stars!" Isla said with a giggle. Both Sabrina and Peregrine glanced down at her in surprise.

"What did you say?" Sabrina asked.

The little girl tapped the paper. "Stars! I know where stars are."

"You do? Where?" Peregrine asked.

She climbed down off the chair and started to leave. Peregrine and Sabrina followed her until they reached the music room. No one else was inside. The circular room was decorated with gold wainscoting and pastoral scenes of plump sheep and buxom shepherdesses lounging on hills. There was a large white marble fireplace, and above it was a vast mirror.

Peregrine looked around, but Isla suddenly tugged on his trousers. When he looked down at her, she pointed upward. He and Sabrina both tilted their heads back to see the ceiling, which was covered in dark-blue paint and hundreds of gold stars.

"My God," Peregrine chuckled. "I believe we have the real genius here. Who knew the little mite was a master of riddles?" He bent to scoop the child up and whirled her around as a reward. Sabrina gave him an intense look, even as she smiled at him.

Sabrina approached the fireplace and examined around the edges. "Where's the next clue?" She spotted a slip of paper inside the curved neck of a golden swan that was molded to the base of the gilded frame of the mirror. Peregrine and Isla joined her. He put his arm around Sabrina's shoulders as they read the next clue together.

My arrow is sharp, and my aim is true,
But I won't trick or deceive you.
Pale as ash when burning hot,
Yet warm to the touch I am not.

Peregrine rubbed Sabrina's hip, enjoying the feel of her warmth against him. He was truly enjoying himself, and he could see in her eyes that she was too. There was a playful intimacy in this scavenger hunt, and he wished it didn't have to end so soon.

"Arrows . . . Are there any paintings of warriors or soldiers?" he asked her.

"No, I don't think so," Sabrina mused. "At least I don't recall seeing anything. Arrows would be old, so tapestries most likely, but I do not remember any of those with arrows either."

"What of the next part?" Peregrine asked. "What is pale like ash but cold to the touch?"

"Something white," Sabrina said confidently. "But cold, like stone. Perhaps an armory?"

"It's possible. But is there an armory in this house?" Peregrine asked.

"No, I don't believe there is." Sabrina nibbled her lip. "It's the arrow I can't seem to place."

"Wait . . ." Peregrine thought back to the tour of Lawrence's house. "There's a gallery of marble statues. They would be cold to the touch . . . What do you think?"

"It's worth an investigation," she agreed.

They left the music room and walked down the corridor, passing by Rafe and Vaughn, who were whispering in the doorway of the morning room. The two men stopped talking immediately when they spotted Peregrine and Sabrina.

"Papa, we saw stars!" Isla said.

Rafe narrowed his eyes. "You saw what?"

"Stars." Isla giggled, but Sabrina put a fingertip to her lips, and Isla covered her mouth with one hand to silence herself.

"All right, my dear. Where did you see these stars?" Rafe started toward his daughter.

"I don't think so. This brilliant little creature is on our team." Peregrine scooped Isla up and stepped back, keeping her away from Rafe.

"Good luck." This time Sabrina was the one who giggled as the three of them left Rafe and Vaughn behind.

The viewing gallery that held the marble statues was a long room with tall windows on one side and a large set of tapestries opposite them. In the middle of the room were six marble creations. Most of them were easily identified as Roman statues. One toward the middle of the sculptures had a bow and arrow and was far smaller than the rest. Two little wings had been carved coming out of his back.

"It's Eros—Cupid!" Sabrina cried in delight. "A marble statue that is white and looks cold and it also has a bow and arrow."

Tucked beneath the wings on the statue's back was another strip of paper. Peregrine picked up the paper and whispered the words since sounds reverberated in the viewing room. Sabrina bent her head close to his. As he spoke, he brushed back a strand of her hair that had escaped the ribbon holding it back.

Look not west, for that is my test,
The sun rises in my eyes,
Far beyond where the crow may fly.

"If one doesn't look west, one looks east?" Sabrina

guessed. "Which if one thinks about where the sun rises, that is also east."

Peregrine nodded in excitement. "Yes, and if one thinks of something as too far for the crow to fly, it must be the far East . . . China! What of the fire screen in the Chinese drawing room?"

They rushed into the next room and searched the black-and-gold fire screen to find another clue wedged between the folded portions. Sabrina read the words on the paper. The final clue.

This is my last breath, but not my death,
For I am the Lord of Thunder,
Yet no man my gold shall plunder.

"Lord of Thunder . . . You don't think . . ." Peregrine imagined the mighty golden Zeus fountain that was in Lawrence's garden.

"Yes! Oh, we'd better hurry." Sabrina and Peregrine left the room with Isla between them and rushed to the steps of the terrace, then down to the lavish gardens of the Russell house. A large square pond in the middle of the gardens held a tall gold statue that was too big to steal—*which no man could plunder*. The figure of the god was blowing wind from his lips, and only water came out.

"His last breath, but he isn't dead. My goodness," Sabrina murmured.

Rafe and Vaughn appeared at the top of the terrace steps behind them, and from the far side of the house,

Lonsdale and Lysa could be seen. Peregrine saw the other men start to run.

"We'd better make a run for it." Fortunately, he and Sabrina had a head start.

"You go—I'll stay with her." Peregrine clutched Isla in his arms. "Go, Sabrina!" he hissed. With a laugh of delight, Sabrina lifted up her skirts and ran straight toward the statue, where she glimpsed a scroll tucked under one of Zeus's arms.

There was a shout behind her, but she didn't stop or look back. She grasped the scroll and clutched it to her chest as she stopped and breathed hard before turning back to the terrace. Peregrine still held Isla in his arms, but a tangle of male bodies lay at his feet. Charles, Rafe, and Vaughn had all fallen on top of each other on the grassy lawn halfway between her and the statue. Lysandra stood not too far off, covering her mouth as she did her best not to laugh. Charles and Rafe scuffled as they untangled themselves and got up. Vaughn brushed grass off himself in a far more dignified manner.

"Well done, Miss Talleyrand," Vaughn said politely. Charles and Rafe echoed this in mumbles.

Peregrine winked at her from behind the other men and mimed sticking his foot out. He had tripped them to give her a chance. It would have been a close thing if he hadn't.

"Oh? Is it solved already?" Perdita called out as she appeared at the doors of the home leading to the terrace, along with Linus. Behind them, the rest of the teams followed them outside.

"Yes, Sabrina has done it," Rafe said, offering her a grudging nod of respect.

"It wasn't me alone. Lord Rutland and Isla also assisted." Sabrina blushed wildly, while praise rained down on her for several minutes.

"Read the scroll!" Linus called out.

She took a breath and began to read.

Congratulations, riddle solver, you have mastered this task,
And for that glowing victory, our hosts you may ask,
For any favorable prize you please,
But do not ask the cook for peas.

She burst out laughing.

"Peas?" Zehra asked in confusion. "Oh dear, our butler must've run out of proper rhymes."

"Well, he is right," Lawrence added. "For God's sake, do not ask our cook for peas. I can't stand them."

"Well, what will you ask?" Charles demanded. "Make it good."

Sabrina, still flushed, shook her head. "Whatever I would have asked has already come true. You have been so welcoming to me. I cannot thank you enough for that."

Zehra and Lawrence exchanged pleased looks.

"Well, the foal award still stands. And anything that you think of, we shall do for you," Zehra promised her.

"And I shall write a letter to Cedric to tell him who

owns the horse. A split of ownership between you and Rutland."

"I waive my right to the foal. Please give it to Miss Talleyrand." If he could do anything for her, he was happy to give her a horse that if she was able to care for it could be quite profitable and would help her achieve some measure of financial independence. She deserved that, after all she'd been through.

Sabrina turned stunned eyes to Peregrine. He merely smiled back at her, and it sent a wild flutter through her belly. Her midnight masked man was living up to every dream. She could not imagine any man willingly giving up his ownership interest in a potential racehorse.

"Well, it's nearly dinnertime. Shall we retire and change?" Lawrence suggested.

Rafe came to retrieve his daughter from Peregrine's arms, and the little cherub clapped her hands together.

"We won, Papa!"

"I saw that, darling. Next time, you must give me a hint."

"I believe it's called cheating," Charles informed Isla. "And you must never do that for your papa."

Isla looked between the two men and giggled.

"Shall I take her, Mr. Lennox?" Sabrina asked. "She likely needs to rest after all that excitement."

"I will accompany you so we can discuss the matter of the horse," Peregrine added.

"Thank you, Miss Talleyrand," Rafe said, and he shot a warning look at Peregrine.

Sabrina led Isla back to the nursery, and Peregrine stayed by her side as she tucked the girl into bed. The whole time she felt his gaze on her.

"She must be tired, after running about the house as we did this afternoon," Peregrine mused.

Sabrina brushed the hair back from Isla's face and kissed her forehead. She'd come to love the child fiercely.

She rose from the little bed. "She's such a wonderful child. To think, she was an orphan . . . She is lucky to have Rafe."

"And he's lucky to have her," Peregrine added as they stepped back into the corridor. "I've never seen him happier. She makes him glow."

"She does, doesn't she? Love has that effect."

Peregrine's tawny eyes glowed. "Have you ever been in love before?"

"I . . ." She thought of him that night at the ball and how he'd given her what she needed most and now was doing the very same. "I think perhaps I have. What about you?"

A gentle, intimate look settled on his handsome face. "I believe I might have as well." He cupped her chin, and she closed her eyes. His lips were soft and warm as he kissed her, lighting that fire within her that she'd first discovered with him that night beneath the stars. After today's little challenges, she was convinced it was him, even if kisses alone weren't proof enough. Against all odds, she'd found him, and yet she had so little time left to enjoy being with him.

He feathered kisses along her jaw and down to her neck, touching places that made her shiver inside. "Am I mad for feeling so much for you?" he whispered in her ear. "Tell me I'm not alone."

She couldn't deny the truth. "I must be mad as well." She brushed her fingertips along the line of his strong jaw and simply stared up at him. Love at first sight was just a fairy tale. But love at first touch, first dance, first kiss —*that* was something she was beginning to believe in.

"What are we going to do?" he asked her, worry lurking in his bright golden eyes.

"I don't know . . ."

❧ II ❧

Three blissful days passed in which Sabrina played lawn games with the other guests, lounged about on idyllic hillsides, and walked in the gardens. And for nearly every moment, she was close to or with Peregrine.

They'd had dozens of moments to enjoy the quiet together, but also moments where they'd been able to talk more of their lives, of their hopes and dreams, and all the things they both wished to do. Peregrine had a desire to travel, just as she did, but neither of them had had a chance in their lives—at least until now, for Peregrine. For a few brief days, she'd had a chance to dream about a life that would never be hers.

Now Sabrina knew that tonight was to be her final night at the Russell house. The house party was finally at an end. Rafe, Isla, and she would be returning to London tomorrow. Knowing that, Sabrina didn't want to waste another moment with only stolen kisses.

She wrote Peregrine a note and slipped it under his door. Hopefully, he would see it after dinner. Then she proceeded down to the dining room, where the others were waiting.

"It's such a terrible thing, isn't it?" Perdita whispered to Alexandra as the two women stood close to where Sabrina stood.

"Yes, for any man to be forced to enter a loveless marriage is simply awful, but why must he?" Alexandra asked.

"Because he inherited his title as an earl, and now he must do his duty, and there are expectations of him to marry someone suitable. He cannot marry beneath his own title."

"He must be incredibly unhappy," Alexandra sighed. "I wish we could do something."

"I quite agree, but there's nothing to be done." Both women then hushed their voices even more, and Sabrina couldn't help noticing their gazes suddenly drifting to Peregrine. Were they talking about him? Did Peregrine have to marry someone at the same level in society to secure his title with a proper heir? If that was true, she had no chance of ever being good enough for him to marry. It only strengthened her resolve to see him tonight and have what joy they could before she had to let him go.

The dinner gong rang, and she looked about for Peregrine to escort her as he'd done since they'd arrived, but he was speaking to Zehra on the other side of the room.

Lord Darlington offered her an arm. "Allow me. It seems our partners are currently occupied." There was a fondness in Darlington's tone that made Sabrina want to smile. He seemed so intimidating and brooding, yet when one interacted with him, he was anything but. According to Zehra, marriage had changed the notorious rogue for the better.

"Thank you, my lord." She accepted his arm, and they proceeded into the dining room, making small talk as Vaughn escorted her to her seat.

A moment later, Peregrine sat down beside her and murmured an apology. They had been doing their best to hide their attraction to each other, but tonight she felt like everyone could see that her heart was pinned on her sleeve.

"How are you this evening, Miss Talleyrand?" Peregrine asked politely.

"Well, and you, Lord Rutland?"

"Well indeed." She felt him touch her knee beneath the table, and she put her hand on top of his.

"So, Miss Talleyrand, when are you to take ownership of your colt?" Lord Lonsdale asked her.

"Oh, heavens. I'm not sure. I have Celeste, but I shall need to find a place to stable it."

"I'm happy to help with that," Rafe volunteered. "When we return to London, we shall meet with Cedric and see to moving the foal to my stables once he is old enough. There's plenty of room for both Celeste and the new horse."

"Actually, Mr. Lennox, I believe I would like to gift the foal to Isla, since I already have Celeste. She can grow up and learn to ride him if he does not end up becoming a decent racer."

At this Charles scowled. "Oh, now I see your game, Rafe. You convinced Miss Talleyrand to give him to you, didn't you?"

"I did not. How dare you!" Rafe growled back.

Sabrina tensed, half expecting the men to come to blows. Lonsdale broke into an arrogant grin.

"Please, Lord Lonsdale, it's a gift for the child, not for Mr. Lennox." But the two men ignored her.

"Settle this the usual way?" he asked Rafe.

Rafe grinned back, but his expression was dark. "Naturally."

Sabrina leaned in toward Peregrine. "What do you suppose is the usual way?"

He shrugged. "I have no idea. And frankly, I'm afraid to ask."

Lysandra peered around Peregrine's other side. "They will both drink until the first man collapses."

Sabrina blinked. "What? But that is . . ."

Lysa rolled her eyes. "Idiotic? Yes."

"I suppose that's where us men will be after you ladies retire," Peregrine sighed, clearly not in the mood for such behavior. Sabrina wanted to tell him about the note, but hopefully she would have a chance to mention it after dinner.

When the meal was finally ended, the ladies left the gentlemen and gathered in the drawing room. Each evening during their stay, Sabrina had managed to slip away. Even though all the ladies had made her welcome and had formed friendships with her, Sabrina still felt unsure as a governess where she ought to be at times like this.

Zehra caught her arm as she tried to leave. "Sabrina, stay. I enjoy talking with you so much. You need not run off. Lawrence and I view you as a guest, not part of Rafe's staff."

"You really are too kind to me." Sabrina could deny Zehra nothing. She'd become so fond of Lawrence and his quiet, intelligent wife. They'd provided a companionship she wished she'd had while she'd been so isolated at her family's cottage.

Zehra led her over to a settee. "Come, sit beside me." The other ladies gathered to play cards at a table a little ways behind them.

"Now, tell me, will you be staying?" Zehra asked in a hushed voice.

"Staying?"

"With Lord Rutland."

"What?" Sabrina swallowed hard.

"You and . . ." Zehra paled. "Oh heavens, Sabrina. I

thought you and he had come to an understanding and had become secretly engaged. Please accept my apologies for the assumption."

"No, it's fine. I . . ." Sabrina wasn't sure what to say. But she knew she could not admit to having a relationship of any kind with Peregrine. It would make Peregrine and Rafe look poorly in the eyes of the others.

Zehra reached out and clasped Sabrina's hand. "Please say you forgive me. I wouldn't have said it if I hadn't thought . . ."

"There's nothing to be forgiven, honestly."

Zehra artfully changed the subject. "So you are to go to London with Rafe. Tell me, is he really as good a father as he appears to be?"

"Believe it or not, he is. There is something wonderful about watching him and Isla together, like a strange sort of magic."

"Two lost souls finding each other—a man born to be a father and a child who deserves him." Zehra touched her stomach and then leaned in. "I've been thinking so much of babies of late, and if what I sense is true, I will gift Lawrence with our first child soon. We have been at the task quite earnestly." She blushed, and the two women dissolved into giggles.

"That's wonderful, Zehra. I'm so happy for you both."

Zehra's blue eyes gleamed. "I admit, I am rather excited at the prospect. Raising children here in the country would be wonderful."

"You must write to me in London and tell me of how it all goes," Sabrina said.

It would be so good to receive letters from someone she had come to see as a friend. Until this week at the Russell house, she had never realized how alone she felt, but she did feel very lonely. For so long she had been trapped in a quiet, desperate life that she'd never been able to escape from until Lady Germain's ball. Coming to live with Rafe and Isla had alleviated some of that loneliness but not all of it. She would always be a governess, and she wanted to be something infinitely more...just not to Rafe.

"Well, I should retire. I need to be rested for our trip home." Sabrina didn't want to leave her new friends here, but she also didn't want to miss Peregrine if he did come to her room tonight.

The other young ladies gave her warm hugs before she made her way upstairs. She paused halfway up the steps and listened to the men, who were drinking and smoking cigars in the billiard room. She sent a silent thought out, hoping he would somehow hear.

Please come to me, Peregrine. Give me just one more night of joy . . .

"I SEE THE ONLY MAN WHO CAN HOLD HIS DRINK IS Rutland," Rafe said, his glass of brandy sloshing onto the carpet of the billiard room.

"He can hold it . . . because he isn't drinking it," Charles grumbled.

Charles and Rafe had escalated their drinking until both men now leaned heavily on their billiard cues in order to stay standing. The absurd matter of honor was yet to be settled between them.

Vaughn, Peregrine, Lawrence, and Linus all watched this battle, their own drinks for the most part abandoned.

"No, it is Darlington a man must watch," Charles said and tipped his glass toward Vaughn. "He can drink and yet you never see him show a sign of being in his cups. What's your secret, Darlington?"

"Wizardry," Vaughn declared without hesitation. It was such a serious tone that both drunken men turned to stare at him.

"Did he say . . . ?" Rafe began.

"He did," Charles confirmed.

Peregrine rolled his eyes. He was tired, and the thought of continuing to watch this drunken game of billiards left him decidedly uninspired. He also wanted to catch Sabrina tonight. Tomorrow she was leaving, but there were things he still wished to say.

"I am turning in, gentlemen." Peregrine ignored the good-natured insults regarding his constitution as he left the room.

When he reached his chamber, he found his valet had left a note upon the floor. He bent and picked it up and began to read over the message, but then he realized it was not a message from his valet. It was from Sabrina.

PEREGRINE,

We have but one more night together. Please come to me after the lamps have been doused in the halls. You gave me such joy this last week, and I long for one last memory of you.

S.

HE STARED AT THE NOTE, THEN HASTILY COLLECTED HIS dressing gown and a candlestick. He lit the candle and checked the corridor. The lamps had already been doused. She would be waiting for him. He moved silently to the opposite wing of the manor to where the nursery and Sabrina's rooms were found.

He knocked softly on Sabrina's door, holding his breath. His heart was racing, and he felt a strange sense of déjà vu, as though he'd done this before. For a moment nothing happened, and he feared she'd already fallen asleep. Then the door opened, and Sabrina's face appeared in the crack.

"Am I too late?" he whispered.

She shook her head and gently pulled him into the

room, gripping his shirt. When she closed the door and locked it, he set the candle on the table by her bed.

"Sabrina, we must talk—"

"No talking, please. I just want to forget about what tomorrow will bring."

He felt uncertain, but she seemed determined to make him forget about anything but being together tonight. She removed her robe and stood there naked, her long dark hair tumbling down her shoulders in wild waves. He'd never been more tempted in his life except that night at Lady Germain's. Yet that night and this both were so vastly different. Sabrina was real, tangible, not a dream.

"I believe you must take off your clothes as well," she said with a nervous smile. He came toward her and placed his palms upon her shoulders.

"We do not need to do this if you don't wish to."

She leaned into him, resting her head on his shoulder. "Peregrine, I feel connected to you, and tomorrow I must go back to my life. I wanted one last memory with you. I know you are a gentleman, but I do not want a gentleman tonight. Please be wicked with me."

She rubbed her cheek against his chest, and he felt that wild flutter inside him, like a murmuration of star- lings taking flight. He could almost feel their invisible wings fluttering against the cage of his ribs.

"Be wicked?" he echoed, and she nodded. "Why me? Of all the fortunate men you could have chosen?" He had to know. He had never been special. He was no more handsome than some other men. Had she felt this way before she knew he was the Earl of Rutland? Or had this been building from the moment they met when he helped her rescue her horse?

She pulled back a little to look up at him. "It's because you see *me*, not some poor woman who is dependent on others. You make me feel like myself in the best way, like I am home." Her brown eyes held a thousand stories he wanted to spend the rest of his life unraveling, but they only had tonight.

"Then it would be my pleasure." He tilted her chin back so he could lose himself in her gentle eyes. He'd become obsessed with those eyes, how they could light up, burn, shimmer, and shine as she turned playful or spoke with passion. He could watch her eyes forever.

He kissed her softly, but quickly lost control and soon let his own passion flow from his lips to hers. She worked at his cravat, unfolding it then sliding it free of his neck before she started on the buttons of his waistcoat.

"There." She laughed with delight as she rid him of his waistcoat. Then he pulled his shirt free of his trousers and tugged it off over his head.

"I didn't get a chance to touch you before," she said as she ran her palms over his bare chest. Wherever she caressed him, his skin burned in the most sensual manner.

"Before?" he asked in a daze.

"When . . . when we kissed the last few times." She

reached for his trousers, and he was helpless to resist. He certainly didn't want to.

Sabrina had almost let it slip that they had been together at the masquerade ball. Thankfully, he was focused on her touching him, because a moment longer and she would lose her own control. Something about Peregrine Ashby made her a complete and utter fool.

His chest was a thing of beauty, all hard muscles with a dusting of dark hair that she admired as she ran her palms over him. He inhaled sharply as she traced a fingertip over one of his nipples.

"Did I hurt you?" she asked.

"No." His rough and low voice sent a shiver of feminine longing through her. "It feels too good," he admitted. "And I cannot wait to return the favor."

"To me?" She raised her eyes to his in question. He captured her hands and pressed them to his lips, pressing a slow, hot kiss to the center of each palm.

"You wished for wickedness, and you shall have it." He bent and scooped her up, carrying her to the bed and laying her upon it. He pulled off his boots and stockings along with his trousers. She had only a moment to see his glorious naked form before he crawled up the bed to her to lie beside her. She reached out to touch his bare shoulder and then his hip. He chuckled and leaned over, pinning her arms on either side of her on the bed.

"When a man is very wicked, he enjoys teasing his lover. He kisses her in all the places he can reach, places that tickle and make her laugh. Places that fill her blood with quicksilver."

"Show me," Sabrina begged him. She wanted to feel for one moment the way she had that night with him at the ball, like she had a world full of joys ahead of her and not sorrows.

"You have magnificent breasts," he whispered. "Almost too large for a man's hands."

He cupped one breast, squeezing gently before he leaned his head down and took one of her nipples between his lips and sucked. Pleasure shot down her body like lightning, and she gasped, arching up into him. His lips increased their pressure, and she writhed as a wet heat built between her thighs. Then he released her nipple and kissed a path across to her other breast. Only as he did so, he also slid one hand down her body to that secret spot between her thighs. She let her legs fall open, knowing what pleasures would come next. He dipped a finger into her, teasing her. She whimpered in frustration, raising her hips.

"You want it, don't you, my sweetheart?"

She nodded frantically. "Yes, please . . . Peregrine." She needed him to the point of madness.

He captured her lips again, making love to her mouth

while he thrust a finger deep into her. When their mouths finally broke apart so they both could catch their breath, she cried out as he worked her to a fever pitch and her orgasm wrapped around her, holding her to him with invisible hands.

"That's it, my love. Let go and just feel." He moved over her then, his hips settling between her thighs, and then he entered her in one swift thrust. She threw her head back, and he held still.

"I'm sorry if this hurts you. Please, it will pass, I promise," he whispered softly in her ear before kissing her.

"It doesn't hurt," she assured him. He believed her to be a virgin, but she wasn't, and she didn't want him to stop.

"Keep going," she encouraged.

"You're all right?" he asked.

"I am. Please, don't stop." Desire burned in her mind, and she could not think of anything else outside of how wonderful it felt to be connected to him. He withdrew and drove back in with growing intensity. He stretched her and filled her, the sensation of his shaft sliding in and out so exquisite that it brought tears to her eyes.

Peregrine was like a god come to life, his body a divine tool for her pleasure. Fire raced between their bodies. She pulled his head back down to hers and kissed him with a desperation she hadn't wanted to let out. In that moment, as her second climax claimed her, she lost her grip on everything that made her feel sure of herself. She was reborn into a new creature, something that craved this man and the warmth of his body and soul.

He stiffened above her, every muscle rigid as he released himself within her. She held on to him, riding out her own pleasure as it slowly faded. But the way she felt now—the same as she had that night—didn't fade. She burrowed deeper into him, relishing the feel of being wrapped up in his arms and surrounded by his raw, muscled physique. He had branded himself on her tonight, and she didn't care. She would always belong to this man, no matter how much time passed.

She pressed a kiss to his shoulder. "Thank you, Peregrine." He kissed the crown of her hair, the tender gesture creating little flutters through her chest. His breath came hard against her neck as he recovered himself. Then he shifted their bodies until they were both under the covers.

"May I stay with you?" he asked. His tone was so hesitant for a man usually so strong and self-assured.

She nodded and moved closer to him, not wanting any of this to end.

"Good, because it would've taken a lot to get me to leave you now."

He brushed the backs of his knuckles over her cheek and stroked her hair away from her face. She wished the stars were above them, that they were again out on the grass in the meadow, lying side by side and gazing up at the celestial view.

"Sabrina, I'm sure you won't believe me, but the way I feel for you, it's not like I've felt for any other woman."

"I feel the same as you, but please don't say any more. We mustn't ruin this."

He pressed a kiss to the crown of her hair and said no more.

❧ 1 2 ❧

Sabrina was alone when she woke. Part of her was relieved Peregrine had the presence of mind to leave her bed before an upstairs maid discovered them together. Yet Sabrina hadn't wanted their night to end, and now it had. Morning had come.

A sense of melancholy settled over her as she forced herself out from under the covers. She pulled on her dressing gown and began laying out her traveling clothes on the bed. She was dressed before an upstairs maid came to pack her things, and then she went in search of her young charge in the nursery.

Isla was dressed and eager for breakfast, so they came down together hand in hand. Most of the other guests were finishing their meals, and Sabrina had a chance to say her goodbyes to her hosts and the rest of her new friends.

She helped Isla with her breakfast, and Rafe found them in the entryway after they had finished.

"Well, we are packed and ready to depart, if you are prepared to leave," he informed her.

She hesitated, wanting desperately to see Peregrine one last time, even knowing it was a terrible idea.

"Sabrina!" Peregrine appeared at the top of the stairs as if her thoughts had summoned him.

Rafe shot him a glare before turning to Sabrina. "Isla and I shall be outside." He picked Isla up and teased her until she was giggling as they left the house.

Peregrine rushed down the stairs and clasped her hands in his. She should have stepped back for propriety's sake, but they were alone, save for a single footman who was politely looking away.

"Please, let me speak to you." He led her into the library, where they would have some privacy to speak. Once they were alone, he grasped her hands in his again.

"Sabrina, would you . . ." He held his breath. "Would you stay with me at Ashbridge?"

Her heart leapt, and she was suddenly dizzy. "Stay?"

"Yes. I could easily make a place for you. You and Celeste would be cared for the rest of your days. I would shower you with jewels, gowns, anything your heart desires."

Her heart leapt with such joy that it startled her, and for a moment she couldn't breathe. All she could do was embrace the feeling of excitement for what he'd just asked her.

"Yes, I will marry you," she answered quickly, too afraid he would change his mind. Perhaps that other woman he was supposed to marry had changed her mind? Or Peregrine had changed his and had broken off their engagement?

Confusion lit his eyes, and in that instant after she'd spoken, she realized she had made a mistake. He *wasn't* offering marriage.

"Oh . . . Sabrina, I . . ." He cleared his throat. "I can't marry you."

I can't marry you. There were no greater words of pain and sorrow for a woman to hear from a man she loved. Yes, she loved him, and that fresh realization was only more agonizing knowing that he did not love her in return. He was still going to marry that other woman, the one Perdita and Alexandra had spoken of a few days ago. The enormity of what she had so briefly believed she was to have as her future and then to lose it—it all settled over her shoulders like a mighty stone, pressing down until she felt she couldn't stand a moment longer.

"Sabrina," he whispered and reached for her.

She pulled away before he could touch her. "No, please. Do not speak. We both said things last evening, and we should have left it at that. It was my mistake to think that I would be a worthy countess." She hadn't thought until just a moment ago that she might have such a life. Now it had been proven how silly that fleeting hope had been, to be loved and cared for by this man and to love and care for him in return.

"Mr. Lennox is waiting for me. I must go." She started for the door, but he moved quickly, catching her arm, but he didn't hold fast. Her arm slid through his grip until all she had left of him was the brief touch of their fingers before they separated. She fled the library and rushed out to the waiting coach, climbing inside and sitting opposite Rafe. She felt the tears well up, and she wiped frantically to clear them from her cheeks.

"I warned him to stay away from you," Rafe said quietly and shot a gaze at Isla who was staring out the window, seemingly uninterested in their conversation. "I *told* him not to seduce you."

"He didn't," she whispered.

Rafe's eyes narrowed. He didn't want her to defend Peregrine.

"He didn't. Truly. Please do not be angry with him."

"Not be angry? He's clearly hurt you. Of course I'm angry! Men should not go about hurting women, whether by action or by word."

She tried to smile. "You act so gruff at times, yet you are the sweetest man I've ever known, Rafe Lennox."

At this, Rafe chuckled darkly. "Sweet? I'm anything but. However, that is a discussion for another day. Now tell me what he's done to you."

"He hasn't done anything," she insisted.

"Sabrina, I hired you for Isla because I sensed you were honest and trustworthy. Please do not disappoint me."

Sabrina blinked away a fresh set of tears. "I fear you will dismiss me from your service." Isla scooted away from Rafe and crossed the coach to sit next to Sabrina. She hugged herself against Sabrina, trying to comfort her.

"Please don't cry, Brina," Isla said in a woeful little voice. *Brina* was the child's nickname for her, and somehow it only made the tears come harder. She put an arm around Isla's shoulders and hugged her back.

Rafe's harsh gaze softened as he watched them. "I highly doubt there's anything you could do that would make me terminate your employment, but I swear on my honor—what little my brother believes I have—that I will not terminate your position as Isla's governess."

That trust she'd felt from the first moment she'd met Rafe hadn't vanished. She knew he would not judge her.

"Shortly before I met you at that inn, I fled my home. My brother ran out of money, and he and his wife schemed to sell me to a man in marriage to have all of his debts erased. But that man was no gentleman. He demanded that I be inspected, to have my virtue proven to be intact before he would marry me, and he made it clear that my sole purpose in life would be to provide him with an heir. He cared not a whit for my feelings. Naturally, I had to dream up a way to avoid this fate."

A frown furrowed his brow. "Naturally," Rafe agreed.

"That night, I overheard my sister-in-law complain

that she could not go to Lady Germain's ball." She looked down at her hands folded in her lap. "It was a masquerade, and so I put on my mother's court dress and an old mask. I walked to the manor house and danced with the most wonderful man before I slipped out into the gardens with him and . . . well . . ." She didn't continue. Isla was watching her and Rafe intently, trying to figure out what came next.

Rafe's eyes widened with sudden understanding.

"No . . . it can't be. *He* was the man you chose?"

She nodded. "I did not know it at the time, of course. He danced so wonderfully, and I felt so at ease with him. When we walked into the gardens, I felt at peace in a way I never had before. We were together that night beneath the stars, and he was everything I never knew I could wish for, but we never removed our masks or shared our names."

There was a moment of silence in the coach, and Sabrina focused on the pounding beat of the wheels hitting ruts in the road. Rafe considered what she'd said, staring out the window, tapping his upper lip. He turned to look at her again.

"But *how* did you know it was him here?"

"When he rescued Celeste from the mud, I thought he was a land steward. I felt that same ease with him as I had with the masked man."

"But surely that was just your mind seeing what it wished to see."

"True, but I could not shake the feeling. I didn't realize he was the man in the mask until . . ."

Rafe reached over and covered Isla's ears with both of his hands. "Until?" he asked, urging her to continue. Isla tried to push her father's hands away, then gave up and frowned at him.

Sabrina closed her eyes for a brief instant, reliving the memory.

"Until I kissed him again. It was his scent, leather and sandalwood, and something unique only to him. And it was the way he kissed me. I knew at once he was the masked man from the ball."

Rafe released his hands from Isla's ears. "You. *You* were the enchantress in the silver gown. My God."

"I was."

He gave her a rueful smile. "After you left, Peregrine was lovestruck. I'd never seen him like that. He pined after you for months. It took quite a bit of convincing for him to let you go, and I fear I am in part to blame for that. I told him you were a dream, that no one could be as sweet as you seemed to be. It's a funny thing, to be wrong. I'm not used to it. I don't think I like it." He was silent a long moment. "And here? What happened between the two of you this week during the party?"

Sabrina smoothed her fingers over the fabric of her gown. Her throat tightened, and she had to focus on control lest she start to cry again.

"We fell in together so easily, and once I knew it was

him . . . I could not help myself. I wanted to be with him again, to be with him in all ways possible. I knew it couldn't last, but for a few days I could pretend. I just grasped what brief happiness I could before letting him go."

"I understand," Rafe replied, his voice soft and gentle. She'd expected outrage and judgment, but she had to remind herself that Rafe wasn't like other men.

"When he spoke to me this morning, he said he wanted me to come to Ashbridge with him. I thought . . ." She choked on the rest of her words.

"You thought he meant to offer marriage," Rafe finished.

Sabrina nodded. "It was silly of me to think that. He doesn't even know that he met me before. I didn't tell him. I didn't want him to think less of me for being a woman who . . ."

"Was driven to desperation?" Rafe inserted. "Sabrina, he would not judge you any more than I. And those who would are hypocrites."

A flare of hope blossomed in her chest, but like early spring flowers that perish from a harsh frost, her hope wilted away as she remembered just what he'd offered her, and it hadn't been the role of wife.

"Well, it doesn't matter. He only wishes to have me as a mistress." She felt so tired just then. She wanted to curl up into a ball and sleep away the sorrow.

A tic worked in Rafe's jaw, and he clenched his fists

where they rested on his thighs. "You shall not be desperate ever again, Sabrina. I vow it. You will always have a place with Isla and me."

Sabrina's heart fluttered at Rafe's statement. "Thank you, but someday when she is grown and married, she will have no need of me."

"Grown and married? No, I won't allow my little darling to ever grow up, and I certainly won't allow her to marry." Rafe gave his child an infinitely tender look and turned back to Sabrina. "So you and I shall take care of her. Let there be no more talk of not being needed."

Sabrina settled back in the coach. She spoke no further on the matter. Someday he would realize she was right and that Isla would not need either of them. When that distant day came, she would have to find a new path in life.

PEREGRINE STOOD IN THE LIBRARY A LONG WHILE AFTER Sabrina had left him. It wasn't until Lawrence found him that he was pulled from the dark mire of his own thoughts.

"Rutland, is everything all right?" the other man asked.

"Er . . . yes . . . no . . . Christ. No, it isn't." He walked over to a chair by one of the reading tables and slumped into it.

Lawrence pulled a few books off one of the shelves and retrieved a bottle of whiskey from the space behind them.

"You keep a whiskey bottle behind your books?" Peregrine asked.

"Only the best whiskey. With Charles around, I find it prudent to hide my most expensive liquor behind books. And while Charles does enjoy reading, he would never choose these." Lawrence nodded at the books he'd pulled off the shelf and set them on the table in front of Peregrine. A small cloud of dust billowed out from the fat volumes, but Peregrine could still see their spines. They were a collection of census records from the area from fifty years ago. No one would willingly crack open such books. Lawrence retrieved two glasses from a drink tray on another reading table nearby and poured them each a glass.

"Now . . . What's the matter?"

"I made a mistake. I hurt someone I care about."

Lawrence leaned back in his own chair. "Hurt how?"

"I made an assumption, but I was wrong to. I was callous in my disregard for that person's feelings. It was not a thing a gentleman would have done."

"Can you undo it? Or apologize?"

Peregrine shook his head. "I offered someone a position as my mistress rather than my wife. It's not the sort of thing that even an apology on bended knee would fix." He sighed and swirled the brown liquid in his glass. All he could think of then was the pain he'd seen in

Sabrina's eyes as he'd offered her the worst possible insult.

"Ah." Lawrence nodded. "I can see that makes a remedy quite difficult. But I must ask, is marriage not possible?"

"It will be someday when I absolutely must produce an heir, but I cannot stomach the thought of marrying until that necessity arises." Peregrine took a long drink of the whiskey, embracing the burn.

"Why not?" Lawrence asked.

Peregrine shuddered as memories of the unhappy lives of his parents assailed him. "Because regardless of how a marriage starts out, it eventually becomes painful. Marriage is disagreements, it is agony and loneliness. The last thing I wish to do is force that upon a woman I care about."

"Rutland, I think of you as a friend, so please do not take insult at what I'm about to say. You are entirely wrong about the nature of marriage," Lawrence said as he abandoned his glass and sat forward. "In fact, I have never met a person more wrong in the whole of my life, and I've traveled to three continents."

"Well, so long as we're not being insulting," Peregrine said with half a grin.

"The problem is, you are looking at the worst of something and seeing it as the whole," said Lawrence. "If two people care about each other, marriage is nothing like that. Yes, there are moments of pain and disagreement, but friendships and families experience the same thing. Love is the vanquisher of loneliness. It heals pain. You and your wife are in this world together, fighting as one heart and soul."

"Clearly, you didn't ever meet my parents."

"Yes, those who marry for business reasons or lust alone can become trapped—but note that word *alone*. Those who marry out of love, or build upon a friendship? They have all the power within themselves to be happy."

Lawrence stood and placed a hand on Peregrine's shoulder.

"Do not discount it. Trust it. Trust yourself."

❦ 13 ❧

T *wo months later*

SABRINA STARED AT THE PURE WHITE SHEETS OF HER BED and nibbled her bottom lip with growing dread. A second full month had passed, and she had not yet bled. Her cycle had always been quite predictable until . . .

Oh Lord . . . I cannot be.

"Miss Talleyrand?" Nelly, one of the maids, entered the room. "You're as white as a sheet. What's wrong?"

She glanced at the bed and then the maid. "I must see a doctor. One who is known for his discretion. Could you find me one?"

Nelly nodded. "Let me ask Mrs. Hutchins. She would know."

Sabrina was still standing in her nightgown by the window, gazing out at the gardens, when Nelly returned. "There's a doctor named Dr. Givens. I wrote down his address for you." Nelly passed her a slip of paper.

"Thank you." She finally forced herself to move, and with Nellie's help, she dressed in a simple pale-blue day gown. Then she went downstairs and knocked on the door to Rafe's study.

"Come in!" he called out.

She peered inside to see him rifling through papers on his desk.

"I was hoping I could have some time to visit a doctor this morning?"

"Oh?" He abandoned his papers. "Are you ill?"

"I am feeling rather unwell."

"By all means. Go now if you wish. Isla and I shall go to Hyde Park. I can see to her until you return."

"Thank you, Mr. Lennox."

Sabrina retrieved her reticule and hired a hackney to take her to Dr. Givens's office, a red brick townhouse in a nice part of London. A brass plaque on the front door had his name and medical title engraved on it. She rapped the knocker and waited until a butler opened the door and guided her into a waiting room.

"Name, ma'am?"

"Sabrina Talleyrand. I work for Mr. Rafe Lennox. His

housekeeper, Mrs. Hutchins, gave me Dr. Givens's name." She rushed through the explanation, praying the butler wouldn't try to shoo her out of the townhouse.

"Please wait here." The butler left the room, and she glanced about, her gaze unable to fix on anything. Her worries only doubled while the clock on the mantel continued to tick away, the only thing to be heard in the silence. What was she to do if her fears proved correct?

The butler returned and motioned for her to follow him. "This way, ma'am."

She was shown into an examination room, where the doctor was seated at a desk making notes. "Ah, Miss Talleyrand?" He stood and closed the door to give them some privacy.

"Yes. Thank you for seeing me, Dr. Givens."

"Of course. Mrs. Hutchins is an old friend." The doctor was a fit man in his middling years, with streaks of gray at his temples that made him look both dashing and distinguished. Sabrina wondered if Mrs. Hutchins was perhaps more than an old friend of the doctor's.

"If you would lie back on the table for me, Miss Talleyrand."

She did, and despite herself, she started to shake as she remembered the doctor Mr. Booker had brought to examine her. That man, although somewhat sympathetic, had still touched her intimately, and she'd been as uncomfortable then as she was now.

"Now, what ails you?"

"I believe that I might be with child. It's been two months since my last bleeding, and I am rarely off schedule." Shame colored her cheeks as she half expected a hole to open up in the floor and swallow her.

"Yes, I see. Well, let me examine you." The doctor gently touched her abdomen. "Have you had any nausea or felt unusually full after meals where you have not eaten much?"

"I was a little unwell a few days ago, and I have been eating less because I have felt rather full."

"Any sensitivity in your bosom?" the doctor asked.

She nodded and tried to swallow down her embarrassment.

"Pain in the back?"

"A little." She was stunned to think that all these signs might be due to pregnancy.

"I must look at you now. I apologize." He gently removed her undergarments, and she parted her legs. He gazed at her a long moment and then helped her put her undergarments back on. "You may sit up now." He turned to his desk and made some notes before returning to her.

"Miss Talleyrand, I do believe you are pregnant, but it is early yet. Do you know when you last had relations with the man responsible?"

She nodded. "Two months ago."

"Then in seven months you will likely bear a child. But you must be watchful. There is a possibility you will spot blood. It's not something to cause further worry, but you should come see me if it occurs more than a few days. There is also the chance that you may miscarry. You are young and your hips are wide, which does give you an advantage over some women, but you should seek a doctor immediately if you experience pains or cramps far above what you normally experience during your time each month."

Sabrina fidgeted a little as the reality sank in. She was with child. *Peregrine's child.*

"It is not my right to ask, but out of concern for a friend of Mrs. Hutchins, I must ask. Is the father known to you? Will he do the honorable thing?"

For a second, Sabrina didn't know what to say because she honestly hadn't considered telling Peregrine. "I don't believe he will. He is far above my station and only offered an arrangement that I cannot in good conscience accept."

Dr. Givens's face softened in sympathy. "There are many places that take women in your position if you do not have anywhere to go." He returned to his desk and wrote down a few names and addresses and handed the paper to her.

Sabrina tucked it into her reticule. "Thank you."

"Will you be all right to leave? If not, you are welcome to remain here as long as you need to."

"I will be all right," Sabrina assured him, though it felt like the farthest thing from the truth. Her hands began to shake as she left the doctor's house. She had to tell Rafe her news and face losing her position. It was the right thing to do.

Sabrina paced outside Rafe's study for several minutes, her slippers wearing a path in the expensive Oriental carpet.

"Sabrina?" Rafe's frustrated voice boomed through the door, halting her as she passed by yet again.

She clenched her hands together. "Yes?"

"Please come in and sit down. You'll wear a spot down to the marble floor."

She reluctantly entered the study. Rafe was lounging in his chair, his booted feet propped up on the edge of his desk. He had a stack of letters in his lap. He picked up one letter, glanced at the name of the sender, and casually threw it over his shoulder to land in the fireplace behind him, where it began to burn.

"Was that important?" Sabrina asked, staring at the letter he'd burned without even opening.

"What? Oh, no, not at all, just some man I despise. I never read a thing he sends me," Rafe replied, then nodded at the chair opposite his desk. Sabrina sat down on the edge, every muscle in her rigid with anxiety.

"Sabrina, please talk to me. It's abundantly clear that whatever happened today with the doctor has upset you."

Sabrina stared at her feet a long moment before she forced her gaze to his.

"I am with child."

Rafe stopped his casual dismissal of letters and sat upright, placing the pile on the desk. Though she now had his full attention, he didn't seem completely surprised. "I was worried you might be. Is it Peregrine's?"

She nodded.

"When did you and he last . . . ?"

"The house party, but it was only once."

"Sometimes you only need once," Rafe muttered. "I assume you fear I will toss you out?" She swallowed hard, and rage flashed in his eyes. "You have been employed by me for ten months now. I had hoped you'd realize I am not like other men. I'm not tossing you out. However, I do believe leaving London would make things easier for you. It cannot be good to traipse about the city once your condition begins to show. If you wish to have any real freedom for the next several months, we must take you somewhere else."

"We?"

Rafe sighed, and Sabrina realized that yet again she'd assumed that whatever came next she would have to face on her own. "I'm not about to let you handle this alone. We can go north to Scotland. My sister married some Scottish fellow. Decent chap—for a Scot. Has a bloody castle and everything. They would be happy to have us visit. Well, you and Isla anyway. He'll tolerate me. What do you say?"

She was relieved to know she had that option, but it would be her secondary plan if her first plan failed. She'd been writing back and forth with Zehra Russell ever since they'd left the Cotswolds two months prior, and she felt certain she could count on Zehra to help her.

"That's a wonderful offer, but I also thought I might write to Zehra to see if she might let me stay with her. She's been so very kind to me." She didn't tell Rafe that part of her—a very strong part—wanted desperately to be near Peregrine and his home while she waited to have his child. That was, assuming he was there right now.

"Will you tell Peregrine about the child?" Rafe asked.

"I don't know."

Rafe was quiet a moment before he gently offered his opinion.

"If it were me, I would like the woman to tell me. But this isn't my child. It's yours. So think on it and write to Zehra. We can leave at once when you hear back from her."

"Thank you." Sabrina stood. "Truly. You've been a better man to me than my brother ever was."

His face suddenly flushed. "Right, well, go see to Isla. She's been asking for you while you were away."

Sabrina bit her lip to hide a relieved smile and went in search of her little pupil.

❦ 14 ❧

O *ne month later*

PEREGRINE STOOD ON THE TOP STEPS OF ASHBRIDGE Heath, watching the distant storm clouds roll toward him. The gray-and-black froth in the sky was but a faint echo compared to the wild winds and violent rains that tore through his heart. From the moment he had let Sabrina walk away from him, he hadn't been the same. He would *never* be the same again.

He had made a grave mistake, and now it was too late. Instead of going after her right away, he'd sat about moping at his country estate like some fool for months because he'd believed he was right about marriage, but now he realized that living without Sabrina was a worse fate than anything he'd face if marriage to her turned out to be like his parents' unhappy union. He would rather take a risk with Sabrina and pray that their happiness would endure than spend one more day in agony without her.

When he'd finally gone to London to try to find her two weeks ago, he'd learned that Sabrina, Rafe, and Isla were gone. Their butler had politely informed him that they would not be back for many months and he was not at liberty to discuss where they had gone.

With a broken spirit, Peregrine had returned to Ashbridge and buried himself in his work. Thankfully, his steward, Mr. Chelton, had allowed him to become involved in the sheep breeding. But even after a tiring day of work, Peregrine would collapse in his bed and his gaze would drift out to the window and into the night, where a blanket of flickering stars hung so far out of reach.

He was cursed, just as his parents had been. But unlike them, he had failed to take a chance on love. He had failed to prove to Sabrina that he was the gentleman she deserved him to be. And only by losing her had he proven to himself that he was madly, hopelessly in love with her.

He watched as a rider came up the front drive to his house. He feared something was amiss, given the coming storm. Peregrine rushed down the steps and soon recognized that it was Lawrence.

"Rutland, I'm glad to have found you." Lawrence slid off his horse with ease and shook Peregrine's hand.

"Is everything all right?" he asked in concern.

"Oh, yes. Everything's quite all right. It's only that we are having a ball tonight, and our housekeeper realized your invitation had fallen off the back of her desk. She only discovered it this morning." He pulled out an invitation and handed it to Peregrine. "So here I am, the messenger at the eleventh hour, so you wouldn't think we'd forgotten you. It would be a pleasant way to while away the storm, if you choose to come."

Peregrine saw his name and title upon the crisp, thick paper and couldn't help but feel like a lost fool as he thought of how it should have been addressed to him and his wife . . . Sabrina, the Countess of Rutland. But he'd lost that future, all because he'd believed he'd not be able to escape his parents' grim marital fate.

Cautiously, quietly, Lawrence added, "We would love to have you this evening, if you wish to come. We have not seen you these past months, since . . ."

Peregrine cleared his throat, pushing thoughts of Sabrina away.

"Zehra is with child, so this will be the last of our public events until after the birth."

Peregrine smiled, happy for his friend. "Congratulations! When is the child due?"

Lawrence gave a rueful smile. "Not for another five or

six months. I know it is overly cautious—but this is our first child."

"Well, in that case, I wouldn't miss it. I shall be there." Peregrine smiled, but while he would enjoy the ball as a distraction, it would be just that, a very temporary distraction.

"Excellent. I shall inform Zehra you are coming." Lawrence mounted his horse, and the beast danced, eager to leave. Lawrence guided the horse to stay still. "Oh, and, Peregrine, bring a mask."

"Why a mask?"

Lawrence grinned as he kicked his heels against his horse's flanks. "It's a masquerade." He took off back down the sloping lawn and onto the road that led through the valley to his home. Peregrine glanced once more at the clouds, which still rumbled in the distance. Another masquerade . . . Another night to survive with a broken heart.

"IT HAD BETTER NOT RAIN DURING MY BALL," ZEHRA grumbled. She peeked out the window of the bedchamber she'd given Sabrina for the duration of her stay. It was a proper chamber, not too near the nursery this time, which made Sabrina both embarrassed and happy to know she was now a friend to Zehra just as she'd wished to be and not simply Isla's governess.

Sabrina chuckled. "As much as anyone deserves to have the weather dictated by their whims, which you do, I sadly do not think the storm clouds will agree to your desires. They seem quite determined to dump an ocean over us." She joined Zehra at the window and shivered as the late-summer storm moved ever closer.

"Oh well, at least it cannot rain inside." Zehra turned away from the window. "Let's get you dressed."

"I really shouldn't go." Sabrina touched the faint swell of her belly.

"Oh, I insist," Zehra said. "You asked me to let you stay here as your prize for winning the scavenger hunt. Now I'm asking you as a friend for a favor to keep me company tonight."

With a sigh, Sabrina retrieved the old silver court gown that had belonged to her mother. She slid the fabric over her arms and onto her shoulders, and the gown settled into place. A shiver shot down her spine. The silver embroidered bodice glinted, and the hundreds of pearls sewn into the fabric seemed to draw in the light and glow.

"You look radiant. Truly ethereal," Zehra said as Sabrina looked at herself in the full-length mirror. This was only the second time she'd worn her mother's gown. The first time it had gifted her with a night of passion beneath the stars. What more could it give her? Surely there was no magic left in the threads anymore, not for her.

"Here." Zehra placed the silver-and-gold mask in her

hands. Sabrina hadn't been able to part with the gown or mask, and she'd kept both ever since she'd fled from her brother's home. She felt foolish, but some part of her believed the gown and mask contained the strongest memories of that night beneath the stars. Even now, as she brushed her hands down the gown, she could feel and hear everything she had that night . . .

Peregrine's teasing laugh, the way they'd walked together in perfect step in the gardens, how it had felt to lie back upon his coat in the grass and surrender herself to him. Everything had been burned into her heart and mind, each second of the two precious nights they'd spent together. It would never be enough for her, yet she had to make it last, and if that meant carrying the gown and mask about with her as talismans for the rest of her life, she would.

"Let's go downstairs." Zehra retrieved her emerald-green mask from the bed and tied it to her face before she looped her arm through Sabrina's.

They descended the stairs and joined a crowd of eager guests, all in exquisite costumes and wearing masks. Lawrence stood at the front of the crowd, his own mask resting on top of his head as he directed the mass of chattering attendees toward the ballroom. Rafe stood beside him, his mask also pushed back on top of his head, watching the proceedings with an unamused scowl.

"Ah, my darling," Lawrence greeted his wife.

"Has everyone arrived?" Zehra asked.

"Almost. We should go ahead and start the first dance." Lawrence gave Rafe a nudge and shot a look at Sabrina. Rafe dutifully held out his arm.

"Sabrina? A dance?"

"Yes, that would be lovely." Sabrina let Rafe lead her into the ballroom. When they were away from Zehra and Lawrence, she leaned in to whisper, "You don't seem pleased to dance with me. I release you from your obligation if you feel it is improper."

"It isn't that," Rafe said. "I am displeased with Lawrence, but that is a private issue between us."

"Ah, I shall not pry, then." Sabrina was curious, but she knew better than to keep asking questions.

Rafe relaxed once they lined up to dance, and he even managed a smile. Sabrina enjoyed herself for several dances before she finally needed a moment to rest her feet. She found an empty seat in the corner and caught her breath, leaning back and stretching her feet out with a little sigh. The musicians played a few lively quadrilles that had the entire room buzzing with excitement.

"How about a waltz?" someone called out to the orchestra when they finished their last song.

Unable to help herself, Sabrina let her mind and heart drift back to that night at Lady Germain's ball, to how she'd first glimpsed Peregrine in the crowd. He'd looked so dashing in a black mask, almost like a wicked highwayman, yet he'd been the most wonderful gentleman and lover.

Her heart gave a twinge, and she instinctively put a hand to her belly. Would their child favor him or her? No matter what, she believed their child would be a wonderful dancer and a master of riddles. Before she realized it, she was smiling. But the smile faded as something across the room caught her eye. A man in a black domino was watching her. Her heart jolted against her rib cage. She had to be seeing things. *He* couldn't be here. Zehra would have told her if he was coming. She stood up, but her feet wouldn't move.

He continued to stare at her as the waltz began. He was still like a statue, and she continued to question if this moment was a dream or reality. What did he see when he looked at her? To him, she might still be the mystery woman from the masquerade ball and not Sabrina.

Her heart quivered, still wounded. She held this man's child within her, the spark of life created between them, and he didn't even know it. Sabrina was torn between running to him and sinking to the floor in a puddle of tears.

He came toward her, uncaring that he disrupted the path of many young couples as they danced. He halted a few feet from her and slowly extended his hand. She put her hand in his without a thought or word. She dared not speak lest he recognize her voice.

As they began to dance, he pulled her close to whisper in her ear. "I never imagined I would find you again, not after that night." He guided her with such grace and ease, it was as though they danced in a castle in the clouds and not upon this mortal ground.

"These last months have been empty, until I found you. Will you finally tell me who you are?" Peregrine asked.

"No," she whispered, still afraid her voice would betray her. She pulled free of him, the warmth and comfort of his touch too much to bear. She fled the ballroom, desperate for air, and burst out onto the terrace. Rain cascaded down on her, but she didn't stop despite the icy chill of the water sinking into her skin and dampening her dress.

"Wait!" Peregrine's shout came from behind her, but she didn't dare heed him. A hand caught her arm and she spun to face him.

"Please, I can't lose you again," Peregrine said.

Sabrina was glad she couldn't see half of his face due to his mask. Looking at him made her weak, made her want to throw herself into his arms. That was the one thing she couldn't do, not if she wanted to stay strong and survive without him.

"You don't know me," she said quietly, making her voice more breathless to disguise it.

He smiled a little, the expression full of sorrow. "Don't I?" When she didn't respond, he continued. "I have one last riddle for you."

The rain was still pounding down on them, but Sabrina didn't move.

"What is an empty shell that once flowed with life, but

now is shattered, and has but one force in all the world that can mend its fractures?"

She swallowed thickly, unable to speak. She'd never heard that riddle before.

"I don't know."

Peregrine took one of her hands in his and slowly got down on one knee. "It is a man with a broken heart, on his knees, praying that the woman he loves will give him a second chance."

"A second chance?" Her voice was faint now.

"Yes. I should have asked you to marry me that night at Lady Germain's ball. I never should have let you leave my arms."

Her shoulders dropped. He still didn't know who she was. She was still just some mystery creature to him. In a strange way, she was jealous of herself. His hold on her hand tightened slightly.

"Please," he begged.

"You do not know me," she repeated.

"You asked me to make love to you beneath the stars," he said, his voice full of quiet desperation. "That is the woman I would spend the rest of my life with."

"That woman is a dream and nothing more." She pulled her hand free of his and turned away.

"Sabrina . . ."

She halted in her steps and slowly turned, shivering as the rain made her dress heavy and cold around her.

"Sabrina," he said again and stood, holding out his

hand to her. "Be my wife. Be the light to my darkness, the joy to my sorrow. Be my world, my hope, my *life*."

She couldn't move, no matter how much she wanted to.

"You knew?" Her voice broke a little.

"Yes," he said.

"When?"

"My heart knew the day I rescued you and your horse from the bog, but my head didn't realize it until tonight. When we danced, the second I held you in my arms, I knew. It was like coming home. I knew you must be the woman from Lady Germain's ball, but I also knew you were my darling Sabrina. In that moment, I became whole."

"But I heard you were engaged . . . that you couldn't marry someone like me."

"What? Where on earth did you hear that?"

She explained the conversation she'd overheard from Alexandra and Perdita.

"It wasn't me they were discussing." His tone was so honest that she didn't doubt him. "Please, Sabrina, give me a second chance to love you with all that I am."

Her bottom lip quivered, and she knew she wouldn't last a moment longer. She cried at everything now that she was with child.

"Please don't cry—you're killing me." Peregrine stepped toward her, and as if her body had been electrified by the lightning flashing above, she jolted forward, flinging herself into his arms.

He wrapped his arms around her, one hand cradling the back of her head as they swayed, rocking her until all her fears faded away, which only made her cry harder.

The rain lessened into sleet and the heat rising from the ground formed blankets of mist around them.

Peregrine pulled back enough to gaze down at her. "Let me take you back inside. I can't have you getting ill."

She tilted her chin back and looked up at him. "You really wish to marry me?"

"Yes. I'm sorry I didn't ask the right question the day you left. I was a monumental fool not to see what was right in front of me. I vow to spend the rest of our lives doing everything I can to make it up to you."

"That's good, because soon the two of us will be three. And I shall need your help."

"Three?" He stared down at her belly. "You don't mean . . . ?"

She nodded, hoping he would be as excited and full of joy as she was at the thought of a baby on the way.

"My God, this is wonderful." He picked her up and spun her around in the rain until she laughed.

"You two had better bloody well come inside! You'll catch your death!" someone shouted from close by.

Peregrine set Sabrina back down, and they saw Rafe and Lawrence standing in the doorway leading back to the ballroom. Peregrine laced his fingers through Sabrina's, and they rushed back across the rain-soaked stone terrace.

"See, I told you the plan would work." Lawrence nudged Rafe as Sabrina and Peregrine stepped inside.

"What plan?" Peregrine asked.

"We threw this entire ball just for the two of you. We thought that if you could meet again as you had that first time, magic might happen again. And it worked, didn't it?" Lawrence grinned. "I assume we will have a wedding to plan next?"

"Tomorrow, if I can manage it," Peregrine assured him.

Sabrina looked toward Rafe, her heart sinking. "Mr. Lennox, I'm so sorry, but I fear I cannot be Isla's governess any longer."

Rafe smiled sadly. "Yes, I know. I knew once we came here that I would lose you to him. I just didn't imagine it would hurt this much."

He spoke with such sincerity that Sabrina rushed to hug him and whispered in his ear, "You saved me, and you gave me my life back. I'll never be able to repay that debt. But I'll try." She kissed Rafe's cheek and then returned to stand beside Peregrine, who put an arm around her shoulders.

"Thank you, both of you," Peregrine said to the two men. "A man is fortunate indeed to have friends like you."

"Good heavens!" Zehra gasped as she spotted them. "You both must come inside right now." She shouldered past her husband and Rafe to drag Sabrina and Peregrine deeper into the house. Some of the guests had noticed their soaked state, and so Zehra hustled them away from the ballroom and up into Sabrina's bedchamber. Maids and footmen were summoned, hot tea was prepared, and a large tub was filled with hot water.

"Bathe, change, and warm up. Do not worry about the ball this evening. It has served its purpose." Zehra winked at Sabrina and closed the door to give her and Peregrine some much-needed privacy.

Peregrine removed his mask and came toward her. She held still as he untied the ribbons of her mask and then pulled it away from her face.

"You are more beautiful every time I see you." He let the mask fall to the floor. "Inside and out, you are the most beautiful soul I've ever seen." He brushed the backs of his knuckles over her cheek, and Sabrina closed her eyes.

She leaned into his caress. "Am I dreaming?"

"Dreaming?"

"Yes. I've had such wonderful dreams, such wonderful moments like this, but then I wake and you're gone and none of it is ever real. I'm afraid if I blink, it will happen again that you vanish."

The soft smile he flashed at her erased every doubt she had and lit a spark of hope within her.

"If this is a dream, then I am lost in it with you, and neither of us will ever wake again."

He leaned down and kissed her, and that spark became

a wild inferno of joy. The world was full of light and love as lightning struck Sabrina and Peregrine for a third time.

THANK YOU FOR READING *ESCAPING THE EARL*! THE next book in the League of Rogues series is *Lost with a Scot* where Aiden Kincade rescues a princess who washed up on the shores of Scotland. Get it HERE!

DON'T MISS ANOTHER NEW RELEASE!
Get my Newsletter
Follow me on Bookbub

WANT TO READ A GOTHIC ROMANCE THAT HAS BOTH a regency storyline and a modern storyline? Turn the page to read the prologue and the first chapter of *The Shadows of Stormclyffe Hall* where the modern day Earl of Weymouth, brooding and sexy Bastian falls hard for an American graduate student writing her thesis on the mystery of Bastian's home Stormclyffe Hall.

THE SHADOWS OF STORMCLYFFE HALL

PROLOGUE

Weymouth, England, 1811

The crash of thunder woke Richard, Earl of Weymouth. The fire in the hearth was low, the embers no longer crackling, and a cold draft pressed in around him as a storm raged outside. Pulling a loose sheet around his hips, he reached across the bed for his wife, who was still weak from bearing him a healthy son a month ago. His hands stopped short as he encountered nothing but the twisted sheets where her body had lain.

An icy tendril of fear churned in his stomach. She never left their bed when it rained. Storms frightened her. Isabelle usually curled into his side, burying her face against his throat for comfort.

Heavy rain whipped against the windows, the fierce staccato a warning to stay inside. Wind whistled through the room, teasing tapestries out, then back against the walls as though bodies moved behind them. A rumble of thunder seemed to shake the stones of his ancestral home, Stormclyffe Hall.

"Isabelle?" he called out. "Love?"

Only the crash of thunder answered.

Lightning streaked past the window and illuminated his son's cradle.

A sharp cry split the air.

Richard leaped out of bed, the icy floor stinging his bare feet as he rushed to the cradle. Murmuring soft, sweet words, he lifted his son, Edward, tucking him in the crook of one arm, relieved the babe was safe. He never thought he would be the paternal sort, but Isabelle and their babe brought out the tenderness in him.

The town viewed his marriage as a disgrace. Earls didn't marry the daughters of innkeepers. But Richard hadn't cared. He loved her and would do anything to have her in his life.

A frown tugged down the corners of his lips. "Where is your mother, Edward?"

Thunder once again rocked the hall. October storms thrashed the castle and nearby cliffs with a wicked vengeance. Trees were split in half by lightning; the edges of the cliff decayed inward, inching ever closer to the castle. Although the storm this night was no different, something felt wrong. A bite to the air, a sense of dread digging into his spine.

As the baby's long eyelashes drowsily settled back

down on his plump cheeks, Richard assured himself that the baby's linens were dry and Edward was content. He brushed his lips over his son's forehead and set him back in the cradle.

When he stepped back, glancing out the window that overlooked the sea, his blood froze. A feminine silhouette clambered through the rock outcroppings by the cliff's edge.

Even from a distance, he knew with a horrifying certainty it was Isabelle.

It was madness to be outside, alone by the cliffs. She knew the dangers, knew the soft dirt around the cliffs crumbled into the sea. Only the year before, a boy from the village had fallen to his death when the ground by the edge gave way.

"Isabelle!" he gasped, the single intake of air burning his chest as though fire had erupted within.

Before he had time to move, the sky blackened, his vision robbed of light.

When lightning again bathed the rocks, Isabelle was gone.

His stomach clenched with a fear so profound, it flayed open his chest with poison-tipped claws.

Shouting for his cloak and boots, he raced from the room. The nurse emerged from down the hall, her white cap askew, and gray hair frizzing out from under the edges.

"Take charge of the baby!" he yelled as he ran past her.

She nodded and hurried to his room.

His valet, followed by several footmen, raced to his aid, carrying clothes. He snatched them and dressed as he ran, his men right behind him dashing through the deluge.

When they reached the cliffs, there was no sign of Isabelle.

"My lord!" a footman by the edge shouted.

Afraid to look, yet unable to tear his eyes away, Richard stared down to where the man's finger pointed. The black shadow of Isabelle's cloak caught on a razor-thin piece of rock, fluttering madly like a bat's wing. Lightning slashed above them, its terrible light revealing a dark smear beneath the cloak's erratic movements.

Blood. Isabelle's blood. Had she jumped to her death?

"*No!*" A crash of thunder swallowed his roar of despair.

He dove for the edge, wanting to follow her into the frothing gray seas. A cloak smeared with blood. All that remained of his wife.

He'd fought too hard to win her love, her trust. They'd suffered through too much together, to be divided now. He couldn't raise Edward alone.

"No...please, no." The pleading came from the bottom of his soul, torn from his heart.

She was gone.

Strong arms hauled Richard back from the ledge, pinning him to the earth.

"It is too late, my lord. She's gone."

She was his Isabelle, his heart...

Why had she jumped? Had she been unhappy? It

couldn't be that. He would have known, and he would have done anything in his power to make her happy.

"We must find her," he told the men standing around him.

An older man, Richard's head gardener, shook his head. "We can't search in this weather, and her body will be gone by the time the storm ends. But we'll try to find what we can on the morrow, if you wish."

"I do," Richard growled. Despair was replaced with vengeance.

He faced Stormclyffe. Lightning laced the skies behind it in a white, delicate pattern. The centuries-old castle loomed out of the darkness, a defensive wolf with the battlements as its bared teeth.

It didn't matter that his infant son waited in a lonely cradle, eager for the loving touch of his remaining parent.

Richard was lost.

He wanted nothing to do with the life he'd had, the riches, the earldom. He despised it all. Every blessed memory he ever had that reminded him of Isabelle made him furious. She was gone from his life forever. He could not bring himself to dwell on his son; it only cleaved his chest in two. His love, his heart, was being battered against the rocks below.

Jane and Bastian

CHAPTER 1

eymouth, England, Present Day
  Blood splashed against white porcelain, the ruby-red liquid spreading outward in a chaotic pattern.

Jane Seyton hissed, clutching her leg. The cut burned like the devil. She slapped a palm over the sliced flesh, but crimson liquid seeped through her fingers. She set down her razor and reached for the shower nozzle, aiming it at the red streaks, washing them down the drain. A thin trail of red still trickled down the tub's edge, and she blasted with the nozzle again, desperately trying to erase the unsettling sight of her own blood.

She hobbled out of the shower, rummaging through her makeup bag until she found a Band-Aid.

Her room in the tiny inn was quiet, the silence thick

and a little unsettling. She hummed to break up the suffocating lack of noise.

It had been a tiring journey from Cambridge to the small, desolate coast near Weymouth in southern England. The White Lady Inn had an almost macabre wooden sign, a silhouetted woman in white standing at the edge of a vast cliffside, her dress billowing out to sea in a cloud of smokelike swirls. It swung above the door and creaked with the slightest breeze. Despite the inn being situated between a lively pub and a quaint grocery store, there seemed to be a zone of quiet within the inn itself. Her room was a drab little place, with a narrow bed and whitewashed walls.

The same family had owned this inn for over two hundred years, passing it down from generation to generation. It was only natural that the place had seen better days and could use a little work. Yet, the awful silence made her skin tingle. She'd hardly slept last night, jumping at every small creak and groan. Taking herself to task, she'd consciously reminded herself that older places made such noises as the wood and stone settled into place.

Today she was driving up to the old castle-like manor house, Stormclyffe Hall, where she was going to meet the owner, the ninth Earl of Weymouth. After several emails back and forth, he'd reluctantly given her permission to tour the grounds along with other visitors but made no mention of getting access to the house's historical papers. Her dissertation was on the tragic stories of some of

Britain's ancient castles and manor houses, with a particular emphasis on Stormclyffe and its effect on Weymouth. Her committee chair, Dr. Blackwell, had given her two weeks to find sources to supplement her theories on Stormclyffe Hall. Since the last four years of research footwork had been done on this one particular castle, she couldn't switch the focus easily to another location. If she couldn't get what she needed, she wouldn't get Blackwell's approval and she'd have to start her dissertation, for a PhD in history, over completely.

In order to complete her research, she had to find out what actually happened to the current earl's ancestors, Richard and his wife, Isabelle, who'd both died under mysterious circumstances. Rumor had it Isabelle had committed suicide. People claimed to have seen her ghost walking the cliffs. Richard had been found one foggy morning shortly thereafter sprawled in his study, a broken brandy glass next to his body. He had apparently drunk himself to an early grave a shortly after his wife's passing. The locals claimed the earl's spirit was trapped within the walls of his castle, restlessly searching for his dead wife, his mournful cries piercing the air on windless nights.

What Jane hadn't told the current earl or anyone else was the more personal reason for her focus on Stormclyffe Hall. Ever since she'd seen an old photo of it, she felt an almost mystical pull. Lately she couldn't seem to focus on anything else.

The hall whispered to her on the darkest of nights,

with soft murmurs and teasing visions just as she began to fall asleep. Before dawn, she'd awaken, hands trembling with the feel of heavy stones against her palms, her heart racing and lips drawn back in a scream as though she'd fallen from the cliffs herself. What she felt, however, in each and every dream she had lately were hands shoving at her lower back, pushing her over the edge against her will.

The obsession with Stormclyffe had cost her so much already. The months of work on her dissertation were now at risk of being set aside if she couldn't find primary sources. It would be back to square one if she had to pick another castle and start all of her initial research over again, but that wasn't the worst of it. Her fiancé Tim had broken off their engagement and ended their two-year relationship, telling her he found her obsession with the castle "creepy" and that he worried she was mentally unstable.

But Jane's dreams made her wonder if the young countess hadn't jumped but been pushed by...someone. And that was the root of her obsession. The nightmares were slowly driving her mad, and she knew she had to get to the bottom of what happened to Isabelle if she ever hoped to find peace. She wasn't sure how much longer she could stand waking up every night gasping for breath and her bones aching as though they'd been smashed upon saltwater-covered rocks. The last few months she and Tim had been together, her dreams had grown increasingly vivid and terrifying, and they'd woken him up as well.

The beginning of the end.

She would never forget the look on his face, the tightness to his eyes and the way his lips pursed as he'd held out his hand and asked for his engagement ring back. His bags were packed and sitting by the door, and he'd left within minutes of destroying her life and all of her hopes for the future. *Their future.*

With a little sigh, she smoothed her left thumb over the base of her naked fourth finger. Even after four months, she still felt bare without it. A splinter of pain shot through her chest, and she clenched her fist, avoiding looking at her hand anymore. She rubbed a towel through her hair before blow-drying it. She could have used a flat iron to tame the mess of dark waves, but she'd fried that when she first arrived in England and plugged it into the wall socket with a converter that hadn't worked properly. She'd never gotten around to buying another one.

Not that it mattered. Given that her academic pursuits tended to involve panels of older, balding male professors in tweed jackets, she rarely bothered with her looks. Her current mission, though, required a more professional touch to her hair and wardrobe. She figured if she looked fashionable and presentable, it might help further her research goals. Easier said than done. She was fully aware she wasn't the sort of woman men fawned over, but her dissertation depended on access to the earl's family archives, and she'd get dolled up if it would help make sure he didn't change his mind about letting her pry into his papers.

The current earl had proved initially reluctant to allow her access to his family history, but when she'd persisted through a deluge of emails and letters, he'd reluctantly said she'd be welcome to tour the grounds along with other tourists once the remodeling was over. That had been four months ago. Stormclyffe didn't have a website to clue her in on whether the grounds were open to tourists or not, but the remodeling had to be done by now. She couldn't wait any longer. And she wasn't going to take no for an answer on getting into those original sources from the current earl.

A smile tugged at her lips.

Sebastian Carlisle, the ninth Earl of Weymouth. A rich playboy with the world at his fingertips. Of course he was tall, with gorgeous, dark blond hair like melted gold and eyes the shade of cinnamon. By all reports, his life consisted of fast cars, leggy models with perfect hair, and wealth beyond imagining. The man was definitely not her type, but she needed to impress him if she was to stay at the castle and work.

Her internet searches also revealed a fair amount about him, aside from his romantic entanglements, and she'd been impressed. With a PhD in history from Cambridge and degrees in numerous foreign languages, he showed a surprising amount of scholarship. Despite his flashy lifestyle, he'd helped push for preservation of historical landmarks throughout Britain and was a member of the Royal Historical Society.

His town house in London was rumored to have one of the country's best library collections, second only to other collections in aristocratic homes like Althorp, home to the ninth Earl Spencer. Even she had to admit that despite reputation as the most seductive man in all of England, and he might also be one of the smartest.

She slipped into her favorite pair of jeans and a comfortable pair of black boots before donning a thick, gray, cable-knit sweater. Back home in Charleston, the weather would be light and warm, but the English coast was always cold in late October. Sea spray drifted far into town, sinking into her bones through the walls of the White Lady Inn.

Though it was still early afternoon, the sky outside her room dimmed as the low-hanging clouds drifted off the sea, dragging their vast looming shapes through the town and blocking out the sun's illumination. A chill seeped through the glass of the window, frosting the edges with dew that pebbled around the panes.

A sudden knot gathered at the base of her skull, the tiny hairs on the back of her neck rising. The air inside was now as cold as outside. Her breath exhaled in a cottony puff, and her skin tingled with a strange sensation. Her muscles tensed in response as though her body expected something to happen. If she hadn't known without a doubt that she was alone, she would have sworn someone was watching her.

She pushed the unsettling thought aside and retrieved her briefcase and purse. Tucked safely inside were her notebook and the latest letter she'd received last week from Sebastian Carlisle. She'd memorized every word.

Dear Ms. Seyton,

Thank you for your interest and inquiry into the Carlisle ancestral home, Stormclyffe Hall. As its caretaker and heir, I am very pleased that my ancestry has found merit in the esteemed Cambridge halls from where you write.

Your dissertation subject is a very interesting one, and I do see how it might benefit your study to have access to my family's documents, and I would welcome your educated account of my home. However, I am currently overseeing the restoration of Stormclyffe, which includes the preservation of those documents that you seek, and having a scholar under the roof while that roof is being mended might prove distracting for both you and the restoration staff. You are more than welcome to visit once the restorations have been thoroughly completed. However, any access to personal and private papers and documents that are the property of my family are not open for public viewing. Weymouth has an excellent library with plenty of sources you might consider as an alternative avenue for research.

Please feel free to contact me, or the office of my steward Mr. John Knowles, in the future should you have any other questions.

Sincerely,

Weymouth

Jane's heart skittered. *Weymouth*. He hadn't even bothered to sign his usual title "Earl of Weymouth." Just
Weymouth. It rolled off the tongue so nicely.

It had taken a half-dozen letters to his office and more
than thirty emails to finally get his attention. His reply
letter had been very British, polite and yet firm. It was
obvious he didn't want her to come, at least not in her
capacity as a researcher, but only as a tourist. *Ha!* He had
no idea what he was in for. She was *going* to get into those
documents.

The drive to Stormclyffe was beyond breathtaking.
Weymouth was a charming harbor town, dotted with
multicolored buildings that faced the edge of the water
inlets like merry greeters. The forest of sailboat masts rose
and fell as the sea rippled beneath the boats, lifting and
dropping them in an endless waltz that enchanted her as
she drove past. It was a place she could see herself living in
for the rest of her life. She loved the idea of the cozy little
place nestled next to the vast acreage of the Weymouth
estate. She looked forward to leaving Stormclyffe on little
breaks to pop down to the city and eat at the local pubs or
visit the little shops and historical sites.

She drove past Weymouth Beach. The jubilee clock at
the edge of the parking lot separated the beach from the
shops and businesses. Its blue-and-red painted tower held
the clock aloft for the residents to see the time at a
distance. It painted a beautiful image, the clock at the
edge of the shore, facing both sea and village. It stood as a

silent sentinel over the flock of tourists that frolicked on the sand and in the shallows.

The twenty-minute drive to the estate took her on a narrow road that paralleled the edge of the coast. Although it was October, the grass was still green on the hillsides, and storm clouds were only a vague outline on the horizon. The landscape gave way to a slowly rising hill and a mass of distant trees, gnarled and knotted together tight as thorns. Just beyond was a glimpse of the castle. It was a massive edifice that stood stark against the sky and trees, towering over the fields, and she couldn't help but stare.

The countless photographs she'd collected over the years hadn't prepared her for the raw beauty and power of the structure. The worn battlements were still fully intact, facing the sea like warriors, ever defiant in the face of nature's force on the coast. The steep cliffs merely half a mile from the castle loomed, dark and threatening.

No fence lined the cliff edges. No warning signs guided visitors away except one that read PRIVATE PROPERTY. HEAVY FINES FOR TRESPASSING. She repressed an achy shiver as a cloud stole across the sun's path, dimming all light.

The gray stones of Stormclyffe stood stalwart and proud, challenging her to drive closer. The road turned to gravel and thinned even more, leaving only enough space for her car.

Sheer desolation seemed to pour off the structure as

she pulled into the castle's front drive. If not for the five work vehicles that obviously belonged to various handymen, she would have thought the castle was devoid of all life.

Strands of hair stung her face as the wind whipped it about. There was an unsettling silence on the grounds, like something unnatural muffled the sound of the sea. No crashing waves, only the violence of the wind against the castle's stones.

The house seemed to be wrapped in an invisible layer of thick wool, where sight and smell were dulled. The wind's icy fingers crawled along her shoulder blades and dug into her hair, making her tense. The castle walls were pitted with small chinks in the stones like fathomless obsidian eyes that stared at her, sized her up, and found her wanting.

The hairs rose on the back of her neck. The eerie sensation of eyes fixed on her back sent a cold wave of apprehension over her skin. She whipped around to look at the deserted landscape, suddenly fighting off a rush of panic at being alone out here.

Her heartbeat froze for a brief moment. A woman in a long white nightgown, hair loose down to her waist, stood hesitantly on the cliff's edge, half turned toward the sea. She stared at Jane. Her skin was grayish, and her eyes were shadowed with black circles as though she hadn't slept in years. Something wasn't right about the way she looked, or the fact that the nightgown looked far too old in style for any modern woman to be wearing. Not to mention a woman in a nightgown in broad daylight wasn't right either...

Sadness filled Jane's chest, choking her. It was as if she were infused with the same lonely desperation evident on the woman's face. Surprisingly, Jane felt no fear, merely the overwhelming grief that had come the moment she locked eyes with the woman. As though pulled by an unseen force, she took a step in the woman's direction. The skies above darkened to a black, thunderous storm on the verge of breaking. Before she could get any closer, black roots burst forth from the rocks below the woman's slippered feet, winding up her calves and digging into her skin like thorns.

Jane had no time to react—her breath caught in her throat as the woman's eyes widened. Jane struggled to move, but her body wouldn't obey. Every muscle was tensed and yet frozen like stone. The woman opened her mouth, a silent scream ricocheting off the insides of Jane's skull. Then the thorny roots pulled her off the edge of the cliffs and into the sea.

"No!" A gasp escaped Jane's lips, barely above a whisper. Her skin broke out in goose bumps, and she shook her head, trying to clear it of what she'd just seen. Her hand shot to clutch her necklace, a pendant gifted to her by her grandmother.

Before she could even run to the edge, a voice cut

through her shock. "She isn't real. Just a phantom." The quiet voice intruded on her terror.

She glanced over her shoulder. A handsome man in his mid-thirties dressed as a gardener approached, carrying a pair of huge shears. The sight was so unexpected after what she'd just witnessed that she wasn't quite sure how to react. Brown eyes studied her with a mixture of pity and concern.

"What did you say?"

The man sighed, set his shears down, leaning them against his knee while he rubbed his palms on his brown work pants. "What you saw there, was the lady in white. She's haunted these cliffs since her death."

Her death? The woman she'd just seen was a...ghost?

"You believe in ghosts?" Jane turned her face once more to the cliffs.

The gardener turned his head toward the sea, his eyes focusing on something from the past. "I believe that evil leaves its mark on a place. Burns itself in the stones so deep that only something truly pure and good can get it out. These old stones have so much evil buried in them, I doubt the castle will ever rest. It isn't safe here, not for you." The gardener bent to pick up his shears again. "You should go, return to wherever you've come from, and forget this place."

She swallowed, a metallic taste still thick in her throat, focusing back on the gardener. "How often have you seen her? The lady in white?" Even as she spoke, the image of the woman's face flashed across her mind, and a chill swept through her entire body. She rubbed her hands over her arms.

He shrugged, eyes facing the cliffs as he answered, "She appears there on the cliffs whenever her kin return home."

She looked toward the hall, trying to bury the memory of sorrow and fear on the ghost's face. Anyone else might have been panicking after having just seen what she'd seen. But the nightly visions plaguing her had slowly forced her to accept that there were things beyond her explanation. Like ghosts.

"So the earl is here?" The earl was in residence. This was good news. She had been a little worried that he might be monitoring the estate from London.

"Yes. Arrived a seven months ago. Been trying to restore the place. Not much good will it do. The ghosts are stirring again. He's upset the balance."

"The balance?" A sense of warning niggled at the back of her head, but she forced herself to ignore it—and to ignore the sense that she was losing her mind.

The gardener appeared to really see her for the first time. "The balance. Between the evil and the good. Evil rules the castle. Stalks the halls and torments those who dare to live inside."

Icy fingers raked down Jane's back.

"Is Lord Weymouth in danger? Being in the house?" It

only occurred to her after she asked that the gardener might be right, and *she* might be in danger, too.

The gardener looked out to sea, his eyes dark. "I don't know. But if you plan to stay here, watch yourself, miss. Evil isn't always what you'd expect. It can take many forms." His voice dropped. "Many forms."

He turned and walked away. The momentary comfort his presence provided her vanished as she gazed upon his retreating form.

She wanted to know what he meant, but she doubted she'd get much more from him. She turned her attention back to the castle. The high windows reflected the sunlight as it started to peek out from the clouds.

The image of the lady in white flashed through her mind again, blinding her to the present for a brief instant. Her heart clenched in sadness, and fear rippled through her in tiny little waves, enough to keep her on edge. Had she witnessed a true apparition, or had her own imagination run away with her? She'd half hoped her dreams of being pushed from the cliffs had been only nightmares, yet that woman looked so familiar.

She had always believed in supernatural things. She was no longer a practicing Catholic in the churchgoing sense, but her faith was strong enough that she respected the truth that there were things in this world she couldn't understand. Like ghosts. And now she was going to enter a place bleeding with evil. She reached up to clutch the medallion of the archangel Michael that hung around her neck. The metal was warm from lying against her skin. It was a small comfort in the face of the looming castle and the fears of what might lurk in its shadows.

WANT TO KNOW WHAT HAPPENS NEXT? GRAB IT HERE!

Lauren Smith is an Oklahoma attorney by day, author by night who pens adventurous and edgy romance stories by the light of her smart phone flashlight app. She knew she was destined to be a romance writer when she attempted to re-write the entire *Titanic* movie just to save Jack from drowning. Connecting with readers by writing emotionally moving, realistic and sexy romances no matter what time period is her passion. She's won multiple awards in several romance subgenres including: New England Reader's Choice Awards, Greater

Detroit BookSeller's Best Awards, and a Semi-Finalist award for the Mary Wollstonecraft Shelley Award.

To Connect with Lauren, visit her at:
www.laurensmithbooks.com
lauren@laurensmithbooks.com

facebook.com/LaurenDianaSmith
twitter.com/LSmithAuthor
instagram.com/Laurensmithbooks